Calypso Warrior

a novel by

Ken McGoogan

Robert Davies Publishing

MONTREAL—TORONTO

ISBN 1-895854-38-5

This book may be ordered in Canada from
General Distribution Services,

☎ 1-800-387-0141 / 1-800-387-0172 FAX 1-416-445-5967;

in the U.S.A., dial toll-free 1-800-805-1083;

or call the publisher, toll-free throughout North America:

1-800-481-2440,

or FAX (514)481-9973.

The publisher takes this opportunity to thank the
Canada Council and the *Ministère de la Culture du Québec*
for their continuing support.

Dedicated to

Sheena, Carlin and Keriann

and to

Anglophone Montrealers,

wherever you may be

TABLE OF CONTENTS

AUTHOR'S NOTE

I am indebted to Alliance Quebec and its ex-president Royal Orr for my protagonist's public reaction to a fictional firebombing. To Steven Nowell, once a Montreal bookseller, I owe the notion of launching a civil-liberties campaign in response to repressive language laws. For the rest, Calypso Warrior is a novel. All characters are fictional. But I'd especially like to stress that my hero, David Nelligan, is NOT based on either Mr. Orr or Mr. Nowell.

1 / AN EXPLOSIVE PROLOGUE

"Daddy, pay attention! Suzanne's cheating."

"I'm not cheating, Emile. You are."

One, two, three. The ringing stopped.

January, 1989. Old Orchard Avenue in west-end Montreal. Having popped an old favorite cassette into the tapedeck, David Nelligan lay sprawled on the living-room carpet, playing Triple Yahtzee with the kids. Eight-year-old Suzanne had rolled a straight flush and big-brother Emile maintained she'd taken an extra turn.

David said, "Shhh!" And waited. Lately he'd been getting threatening phone calls — a man's voice suggesting in flawless English that if he knew what was good for him, he'd get out of Montreal, click.

Again the phone began to ring. That was the signal: three rings, stop and start. David nodded his okay and Emile picked up the receiver. The boy's eyes went wide: "Daddy, it's Uncle T."

David took the phone. "Tolbert, what's up?"

"The bookstore's on fire."

"What? Tolbert, if this is —"

"No joke, David. Just got a call from the janitor across the street. Said he hears this noise, like a small explosion. Looks outside and the store's glowing red."

"The fire department?"

"They're on the way."

David banged down the phone and Time went strange. Racing to the hall cupboard felt like running underwater. In slow motion, he grabbed his ski jacket. The kids stared up at him, wide-eyed, silent. He'd leave them with the woman next door. No, wait. Tonight she played bridge. And Arianna wasn't due home for another hour. Snapping back into real time, David cried: "Bookstore's on fire! Grab your coats!"

David led the kids out the back door, down the icy steps and into the garage. Piled them into his rattletrap Chevy, swung north out of the alley — "Daddy, that's not allowed!" — and roared east along

Sherbrooke. Traffic was light, the boulevard free of snow. At red lights David just slowed down and honked before speeding through. Managed the drive in twelve minutes.

The bookstore was situated on Milton Street in the McGill ghetto and fifty or sixty people had gathered out front, university types. They stomped their feet and flapped their arms against the cold. Two firetrucks sat in the street, red lights flashing in circles. Half a dozen firefighters paraded around in yellow raincoats and black hip-waders, waving their arms, telling people to move back. Others were putting away hoses.

David pulled onto the sidewalk. He told the kids to stay in the car, then jumped out and shoved through the crowd. A firefighter tried to stop him. David hollered, "I own the store!"

The man let him pass.

The front door hung loose off its hinges. The bookstore stank of fire and water and something else. Gasoline? Fire had swept through the front room, reduced most of his stock to black tissue paper. A few dozen hardcovers lay in soggy piles on the floor. The shelving was beyond salvage. David felt weak in the knees. He kept moving.

Fire had gutted the back room, too. The damage was even worse. David stumbled over to his desk, found it piled high with charred rubble. Same with the chair behind it, no place to sit down. Leaning against the desk, David noticed that a side window had been smashed. He stepped towards it and kicked something. Looked down and saw a pipe. Three inches across, maybe two feet long, stoppered at both ends.

He waved a fireman over, pointed.

"Tabernaque!" the man cried. *"Une hostie de bombe!"*

Firefighters scrambled out of the store with David right behind them. The crowd had grown to seventy or eighty people, most of them crowded onto the far sidewalk. Tolbert had arrived. He stood arguing with a firefighter — "I'm an ex-partner!" — trying to get past. David hurried over and, wordlessly, the two men hugged. Emile and Suzanne emerged through the crowd and David let them stay, each of them holding a hand.

After a while, the bomb sqaud arrived — three men wearing masks and padded suits. They carried sandbags into the bookstore.

"Daddy, what are they doing?"

"I don't know."

"They pack those bags around the pipebomb," Tolbert said. "Then they detonate it. Ka-boom!"

Twenty minutes later, when it came, the explosion rattled windows in the apartment building behind them. Suzanne started to cry. As David kneeled to comfort her, Emile looked over at him, troubled, and said, "Daddy, what if you'd been working late?"

2 / ISABELLE'S GAMBIT

Three weeks later, Isabelle Garneau reduced the firebombing and its aftermath to the status of second-biggest problem. This David discovered in a convenience store around the corner from his home. He'd bought milk and bread and three cans of tomato soup, then picked up a copy of *La Nouvelle de Montreal*. Standing in the check-out line, waiting his turn, he opened the newspaper. There, at the top of Page Five, was a three-column photograph of Isabelle Garneau, inset with a one-column mugshot of himself: the notorious David Nelligan.

To the left of this photo, a sixty-point, bold-face headline blared, *en francais:* "Québécoise novelist reveals secret past of Anglophone arson suspect."

The store began to spin. David grabbed the counter. The woman at the cash said, "You okay?"

"Just over-heated."

David sat down on a pile of old newspapers, hung his head between his knees and breathed deeply. Then, partially recovered, he reopened *La Nouvelle* and translated as he read....

Isabelle Garneau, the celebrated Québécoise novelist, has revealed that one of her books paints a startling portrait of David Nelligan, the Anglophone activist suspected of fire-bombing his own bookstore.

Delaronde, considered one of Quebec's leading feminist writers, said her novel *Le Diable Entre Nous* tells the true story, thinly disguised, of eighteen months she spent living with Nelligan.

The novelist said she felt compelled to reveal this now because of the furore surrounding the recent explosion and fire at Calypso Canada Books. "David had a lot of strange ideas," Delaronde said, "as anyone who reads my novel can see. Still, I wouldn't have thought he'd set fire to his own bookstore. Maybe the police know something I don't."

Le Diable Entre Nous, Delaronde's sixth novel, takes place in Greece. It tells the story of a sordid love triangle involving two English Canadians and a Québécoise.

The man in the middle is an arrogant male chauvinist for whom one woman is not enough. He speaks French and professes sympathy for the Québécois struggle, Delaronde said, but is sadly incapable of understanding the narrator's legitimate desire to help create an independent Quebec.

Delaronde said she met Nelligan in the mid-seventies, when she taught briefly at Concordia University, and travelled with him to Greece. "David never knows when to quit," she said. "I hope he's learning something from all this."

Delaronde's publisher, Editions Dufort, is preparing a second printing of *Le Diable Entre Nous*, which appeared originally in 1979. It will be available in Montreal bookstores within six weeks. The novel is also being translated into English, Delaronde said, and will appear in that language next fall.

As David read and re-read the story, he realized that with this, Isabelle's gambit, the tabloid's on-going smear campaign had reached a climax.

Originally, *Le Diable Entre Nous* had disappeared without a trace — too vindictive for the literary, too flashy and experimental for the strictly political. Despite previous successes, Isabelle had been unable to find a translator. And as long as the novel existed only in French, David had remained immune to its vitriol. Likewise, Arianna. Of their friends and relations, only Tolbert knew the book existed. And he didn't have enough French to read it.

Now, however, under the guise of rushing to his defence, Isabelle had found a new way to assault him. And simultaneously to damage, not incidentally, the cause with which he'd lately become identified: the right to live in English in Quebec.

David felt nauseous. Again he hung his head between his knees. During the past few days, ever since the French tabloids had gone on the offensive against him, he'd been feverishly studying libel law. And so he understood that Isabelle had seized a new opportunity. By responding to the firebombing, he'd become a public figure. That meant Isabelle could identify him with a vicious "fictional" portrait and, if charged with libel, plead fair comment.

Even in French, she'd never dared to identify him publicly as the neanderthal boor of *Le Diable Entre Nous*. Now, the novel would surface in English. Not quietly, but with headlines that linked the book directly to him: "Two-timing Anglophone Repudiates Distinct Society."

What could he do? Run shouting along St-Catherine Street: "Wait! This is a set-up! It's a pack of lies, a vituperative tirade by an angry ex-lover! I'm not really an egotist, a liar, a hypocrite and a coward! I'm not really a slavering, anti-French brute!"

That was when David got his Big Idea, while sitting on newspapers in the *dépanneur* — the idea of writing a political allegory. He'd tell the world what really happened while drawing attention to the parallels. Why hadn't he thought of this before? Just as ethnic nationalists wanted to eradicate the English community, so Isabelle was bent on destroying him personally. The former hid behind a trumped-up need to preserve the French Fact, the latter behind the sanctity of literary fiction: "What? You've got a quarrel with literature?"

His mind whirling, David paid for his groceries and headed for home. He strode along Sherbrooke oblivious to the cold and blowing snow, thinking: *Forget the libel suit, worry about that later.* Instead, he'd fetch those cardboard boxes out of the basement. They were full of notebooks and letters from his days with Isabelle. In those boxes he'd find the truth. He'd vindicate himself and his cause by turning that truth into allegory.

3 / A NASTY THREAT

That afternoon, in the house on Old Orchard Avenue, David Nelligan leaned across his paper-strewn desk, blew a hole in the ice on the window and peered through it. Snow was lightly falling — scattered, awkward flakes that marked the stuttering end of a two-day storm.

With Arianna and the kids gone, better safe than sick-with-worry, he'd dragged his desk into the front room. Now he looked north up Old Orchard. A snowplow had cleared one lane while he'd napped, but the sidewalks remained waist deep in snow. Near Sherbrooke, half a block away, three people in duffle coats were digging out a small van. But of course: Friday night. They were in their mid-twenties and, blizzard or no blizzard, they were going out.

A mother and two children came slip-sliding down the street towards him, the woman watching for cars. David sighed and let fall the curtain. How was he going to tell Arianna the latest? That *Le Diable* would be appearing in English? *The Devil Among Us.* He still didn't know. Even so, he reached across the desk and put the phone back on the hook. Coffee. He needed coffee.

David scuffed down the hall, heard the sound of his slippers on hardwood, tried to ignore the emptiness of the house. He found himself remembering another Friday evening, what? a dozen years before? Yes, 1977. Before the kids. Before the book-store, even. He and Arianna were renting a five-room flat a few blocks away. They'd recently returned from Greece and Africa and David had landed a job at *The Montreal Standard,* where as a newly hired copy editor he worked the graveyard shift, midnight to eight in the morning.

Arianna woke him early that evening. She was heading downtown to attend a lecture at the *Université de Montréal,* some hot-shot interior designer from France. The streets were bad enough — this was mid-winter — that Arianna had decided to take a bus. Already she was late. She kissed him goodbye and was gone.

David showered, pulled on his jeans and a sweatshirt and devoured a dinner-breakfast of toast and scrambled eggs. Afterwards, as he settled into his favorite armchair with a separatist classic — White Niggers of America by Pierre Vallières — the telephone rang. Probably the copy-chief at *The Standard,* wanting him to report early. David decided not to answer. Might also be Emmanuel Tolbert, he realized, with a more agreeable proposition, or maybe Arianna stranded at a bus stop. He caught the phone on third ring.

"*David? C'est moi.*"

"*Isabelle!*" He hid his disappointment. "*Ça va?*"

"I've got news," she said, continuing in French. "Can I come over?"

"Have you seen the roads?"

"I'll take a taxi, no problem. Be there in half an hour."

"Arianna's out."

"That eco-designer? Who'd have guessed? You'll have to face me alone."

David laughed weakly. He hadn't been intimate with Isabelle for months and liked it that way. Recently, though, she'd begun dropping hints. Would she never get the message?

Unable to concentrate on his book, David was sifting through his cassette tapes, hunting an old favorite Tolbert had given him, and telling himself that tonight would be fine, when the door bell rang and here she was, covered in snow and carrying a brown paper bag. Smiling brightly, Isabelle thrust the bag at him.

"Champagne!" he said. "*O-la-la!*"

"That's what took me so long."

They pecked each other on both cheeks. David took Isabelle's floor-length black coat, shook it free of snow and hung it on the rack beside the door. "What are we celebrating?"

Isabelle swirled into the room. "Remember that translator I told you about?"

"She's going to do *Les Incantations!*"

"No, even better. Both *Incantations* and *Le Malin.* A matched set."

"Isabelle, that's great!"

While David popped the cork and located wine glasses, Isabelle talked excitedly about the translator, who'd handled novels by the likes of Jacques Godbout, Marie-Claire Blais and Hubert Aquin. David toasted her good fortune and then, having made all the right noises, took the plunge: "We've got news, too."

Incredibly, the phone rang.

David picked it up but said nothing.

"Nelligan? Don't you dare hang up."

"Wouldn't dream of it, chief."

The Standard needed him early. David said no problem. Having hung up, he turned to find Isabelle scrutinizing a pen-and-ink sketch Arianna had done in Africa, two women at work in a field. "Here we can see why, David, most of the time I like Arianna better than you."

Isabelle had switched to French and David went with her: "Sometimes I like her better than me, too."

Isabelle ignored him, continued moving around the room, studying Arianna's sketches and paintings. "She's not as verbal as we are, but in some ways she's more sophisticated, don't you think?" Isabelle turned to face him. "In other circumstances, she and I might have been good friends."

"I thought you were friends."

"We have moments of friendship. But the triangle's awkward. It means denying any physical feelings I have for you, David, pretending they don't exist — and then I feel not just frustrated but hypocritical."

In English, David said, "More champagne?"

Isabelle handed him her glass but kept talking. "Of course I'm Arianna's friend — and a better friend than you realize, because I see her clearly. I understand her manipulations and still I like her."

"Let's not get into this tonight," David said. "Down the hatch."

Isabelle followed him back into English: "Let's not get into what, David?" She took a swallow of champagne. "Women are underhand with each other, that's all I'm saying. We're taught to see each other as rivals. And when you really are rivals, when two of you love the same man, even though you've both suffered through his actions, well, you use your resources. You say things like, 'I've never had a baby, and if Isabelle has your baby, I'll leave.'"

Isabelle held out her glass but David just stared. Finally, shaking his head, he poured. "Sometimes, Isabelle, you really are uncanny."

"Uncanny?" She repeated the English word, savoring the sound of it. "How so?"

"Arianna and I are going to have a baby."

Isabelle swallowed her champagne slowly: "You're joking, of course."

"No, Isabelle, that's our news. I hope you're happy for us."

"Happy for you, David? My first impulse is to say, 'Now that Arianna's pregnant, can I have a baby, too?'"

"Isabelle, please don't."

"You're right, David. I'm forty-three. Too old to have another baby." Isabelle began circling the room, talking to the walls. "Not Arianna, though. Oh, no. It's not too late for Arianna."

"I know it's a shock."

Talking steadily, Isabelle retrieved her coat: "In Greece you had me in a double bind. I knew I could get pregnant and tell you afterwards, and that you'd love the child. But even I couldn't do that."

"Do you want me to call you a cab?"

"Now you're cutting me out of your life." Isabelle pulled on her coat. "Do you remember, David, that not so long ago I suggested we agree to a five-year moratorium on writing about each other?" She picked up her champagne. "I've never understood why you refused."

"Because you're the famous one. A moratorium wouldn't have been fair to you."

"Fair to me?" Isabelle tossed her champagne in his face. "That's what I think of your fair-to-me!"

David wiped his face on his sleeve. He knew that Isabelle's script called for him to respond physically, perhaps in kind. Instead, he shook his head and dropped his hands to his sides. "Isabelle, I don't know —"

Isabelle spun on her heel and strode away down the hall. At the door she turned and faced him, her eyes slits, her voice cold: "You'll pay for this, David Nelligan. You'll pay for this."

4 / NELLIGAN'S TUMBLE

Returning to the living room, mug of coffee in hand, David Nelligan noticed the mess. Usually he kept the place neat and tidy. That morning, stunned by the subtle ferocity of Isabelle's latest offensive, he'd ventured into the dank, dirt-floor basement and retrieved a dozen cardboard boxes from jerry-built shelves.

Having lugged these boxes up creaking stairs and dragged them into the living room, he'd found unexpected riches: notebooks from the early days in Montreal, official documents from the freighter cruise, and from Greece, not only the letters and journals he sought, but a photo-album history Isabelle had given him.

Now, stepping carefully among the piles, David retrieved this album and brought it to his desk. Sat down and, for the first time in over a decade, began flipping through its pages. Here was Isabelle descending the front steps of her two-storey house in Outremont. Here she was in the town of Ste-Thérèse, where he'd shown her his boyhood paper route. And here, back in Montreal, she smiled brightly and waved freighter tickets from a café in Place Jacques Cartier. She wore a floppy hat that shaded her face, but if you looked closely, you could see the division, the split.

David remembered thinking, the first time he saw her: "The two sides of her face don't match."

Concordia University, that was. What? Fifteen years before? Autumn, 1974. With Arianna, he'd just spent three years in Toronto: two as a journalism student, one as a cub reporter at *The Toronto Tribune.* Now they were back — Arianna at the *Université de Montréal,* studying interior design; himself at Concordia, bent on writing The Great Canadian Novel while earning a master's degree.

As it happened, all the students who signed up for the novel-writing workshop that year were male, and Paul Emmett, who ran the program, decided to bring in a woman. Enter Isabelle Garneau. Emmett introduced her as an emerging Québécoise novelist who'd agreed to sit in and provide a woman's perspective. He rattled off the titles of several of her novels, but even David, fluent in French and aware of Isabelle's reputation as both a nationalist and an avant-garde feminist, had read none of them.

Still, he knew enough to smile grimly when T.J., a would-be Hemingway from northern Ontario, asked as they left the workshop if Isabelle wrote Gothic Romances. David answered, "Something like that."

After a couple of workshops, even the macho T.J. knew better than to take Isabelle lightly. She was too sharp, even in English: mistress of the arched eyebrow and the devastating one-liner. She'd studied at the Sorbonne.

David forgot the split in her face. He admired her wit, enjoyed her accent, and had two or three light-hearted exchanges with her *en francais,* partly for fun, partly to show off to his unilingual peers.

Even so, Isabelle didn't become real to him until his own novel-in-progress hit the workshop table. These sessions, he knew, could be hard on the ego. One would-be novelist — six-foot-five, built like a linebacker — had disintegrated into red-faced incoherence, and another had fled at coffee break and never returned.

Yet, when his own turn came, David arrived expecting adoration: "Talk about comic genius! My god, this Nelligan can write."

And gaped to discover himself surrounded by faint-praisers. Competent, they said, but glib. Too journalistic. Where's the poetry?

Isabelle became real as his defender.

David's use of the first-person was intrinsically dramatic, she said. And look at the humor, the vitality. These early scenes were teeming with life, full of energy: "If Nelligan keeps this up, and the rest of his novel is half this good, you'll find it in bookstores next year."

David believed it.

The novel workshop happened Friday afternoon, and several of the graduate students, himself included, had begun adjourning to the Rymark Tavern on Peel Street. That afternoon, still glowing, David invited Isabelle to join them — though not without trepidation. She was forty years old, after all. An established writer.

To his surprise, Isabelle said yes. And had a good enough time that, the following Friday, she again joined the gang. Soon she was a Rymark regular, just another one of the guys — not all of them from the workshop — who'd push tables together and quaff beer and play word games.

At the Rymark, Isabelle would sit next to David, and sometimes they chatted in French. Early on, against a background of beer and smoke and laughter, and what she called the usual English cacaphony, Isabelle described how she'd launched her career by publishing, in a Paris-based literary magazine, a story set in French West Africa. A Montreal editor had seen it and wrote urging her to turn the story into a novel.

The result was *Les Incantations*.

The book had gone out of print, Isabelle said, so no, David couldn't pick up a copy. But she felt odd, she confessed, passing judgment on younger writers, none of whom had read her work. And the next Friday she lent David her first novel.

A few nights after that, with Arianna already in bed, David sat down to read a while and found himself unable to stop. *Les Incantations* told the story of a disastrous love affair that ended, or rather revolved around, a botched abortion. The work was autobiographical, and so apparently honest it was painful — but in that David saw nothing but courage.

Never mind the subtext. What an eye for detail! What an ear for speech! Pyrotechnics? Isabelle made French do everything but card tricks. At the razzle-dazzle of her technique, the young writer could only marvel, shaking his head. And when, at three o'clock in the morning, he finished reading, David decided that he was in love.

5 / START WITH GREECE

Forget the allegory. That's what I've decided to do. Develop it later. Start with Greece, where no matter what island we'd picked, Isabelle and I would have shared the same lunacy, I know. In 1976, as it happened, we settled on Callisto, an island so magical that even now, thirteen years later, and socked into a creaky house in wintertime Montreal, even now if I close my eyes I can call it forth.

Picture me driving a rented car out of Palamedes, a bustling port city, picking my way through dusty streets choked with motorized three-wheeled vehicles, not motorcycles and not quite cars, seats up front and open boxes in back — the perfect Greek rejoinder to the North American half-ton. Heading south out of the city, I puzzled over the markers erected at every corner, chest-high, mostly hand-made, and realized only gradually that these were shrines.

I remember dry brown hills rolling away into the distance, hills beyond hills beyond hills, all of them dotted with olive trees and lined with worn footpaths winding away to the horizon. And sea-side towns, harbours thronged with fishing boats and streets lined with white-washed houses — white with red trim, white with blue trim, white with green trim, everything white, white, white.

Best of all I remember the village of Apolakia as it looked from the needle-like sentry box that stood on a promontory above the harbour — my special place. Every afternoon, after writing for hours, I'd lean against that needle and stare out over the Mediter-ranean, thinking of Arianna. From the sentry box, too, I'd look back at Apolakia, at the fishing boats in the harbour, the fishermen unpacking their nets. And the town square — really a semi-circle of cafés and tavernas facing the harbour, with the town itself climbing the hill above them, all of it white.

Again I see the Greek men lounging in hard-backed chairs outside the café they'd reserved by force of habit, talking together, waving their arms, pausing to watch in silence whenever a young woman sauntered by in a bikini, American or Swedish or German, here for a week and bound for the beach to sunbathe topless. I see the circular green bench where travellers would sit waiting for the bus to arrive from Palamedes, its roof piled high with boxes and baskets and bicycles, and where every afternoon, having scrambled down the hill, I'd meet Isabelle and we'd swing past the cafés and follow the winding, rocky footpath along the water to the nearest sand-and-pebble beach.

Here's a photo of Isabelle on that circular green bench: blue cardigan, white slacks, tumbling black hair, and behind her a tree bright with red and orange blossoms. It's an early photo, a happy explosion of color in which she looks well-rested, content. I see the two of us later that afternoon, done swimming, sitting at one of the cafés drinking ouzo, chasing down the licorice taste with water while bouzouki music blares from loudspeakers behind us, looking out at the harbour and marvelling that we're really here, really in Greece, enjoying the idea while we wait for the bus to arrive from Palamedes, when we'd order a final glass of ouzo and so give the strange man at the post office time to sort the mail.

From my special place on the promontory, by the sentry box, I couldn't see our flat. But from where I sit now, at a desk in west-end Montreal, I can see it clearly: three rooms over a grocery store on the quietest, most traditional street in Apolakia, where except for us only villagers lived and tourists felt unwelcome. I remember the astonishment of the owner, Marcos, when I made it clear, mostly through sign language, that we wanted to rent all three rooms, the whole second floor — and not by the week but the month.

Apolakia. Our front entrance was a doorless hole in the wall. We'd deke through this hole off the street and climb white stairs to a hall, with more stairs at the far end leading onto the roof. The walls were white. The kitchen was a renovated cupboard with a counter, a hot plate and a sink; the tiny bathroom contained only a toilet. Still, we declared the three rooms a flat. Marcos and I shook hands and downed tumblers of an eye-watering, aniseed liqueur called *raki*, and so there we were, Isabelle and I, settled on the magic island of Callisto.

Our flat wasn't the villa we'd imagined, but neither was the price. Isabelle paid ninety dollars to my eighty-one — we're talking 1976 — so she got her choice of studies and took the larger, which looked out over the tiny street. My own study, at the back of the house, gave me a view of the highway as it wound down the hill into town.

Mostly we lived in the largest of the three rooms: white concrete walls, two single beds, a tiny kitchen table, three hardbacked chairs and a sink. Cold running water. Sometimes, we'd carry the table out onto the porch, cover it with a checkered table cloth and eat dinner there, washing it down with dry red wine.

In *Le Diable Entre Nous*, Isabelle writes of visiting the roof of the house, of lying on her back and gazing up at the stars. She wonders, disingenuously, why I refused to sleep up there with her. Fact is, as she well knew, I was afraid. The moon was full when she suggested this, huge and yellow in the Mediterranean night. And I'd read her novels, every one of them shrieking witchcraft, howling omens and incantations.

I wasn't superstitious, exactly — but sleep with Isabelle Garneau under a full moon on Callisto? You've got to be kidding.

6 / WORKING THE GRAVEYARD

"Okay, mon, I buried it."

Tolbert's voice. David had been punching away at his computer, lost in Greece, wondering whether to change the names now or later, and he'd caught the telephone on third ring. Tolbert's voice brought him back to Old Orchard Avenue and his immediate problem: Isabelle's gambit. As nasty a piece of work as ever she'd concocted.

To Tolbert, he said: "Great stuff! How deep?"

"Well, B-1."

"B-1? As in First City? You call that buried?"

"David, I had to fight to keep it off the front."

Finally, David sighed and said, "How's it read?"

"A straight scalp of the *Nouvelle* yarn. I added a couple of graphs about the libel suit you're launching. Any progress?"

"Not on that front, no." David decided not to mention that he'd dumped the law books onto the floor and started writing about Greece. "This latest twist," he said. "Maybe it's time to change tactics."

"How's Arianna taking it."

"I haven't told her yet. Already she thinks we should move to Calgary."

"You're kidding me, right?"

"She's sick of the threats, the public abuse."

"But Calgary?"

"Says she'd start an interior design business. And I could open another bookstore or go back to newspapering."

"You talk sense to this woman?"

"Don't worry. No way I'm leaving Montreal."

"What about the kids?"

"Someone's at the door, Tolbert. Gotta run."

"I taught you that trick, remember?" Tolbert hung up before he did. But David couldn't get back to Greece. Maybe change the names later? He spun away from his computer and scuffed down the hall to make another coffee. The noise behind Tolbert —

he'd called from *The Chronicle* newsroom — had brought back their nights together at *The Montreal Standard*. What? Early 1977?

David put on the kettle and, while he waited for the water to boil, remembered the night they conceived the bookstore. They were working the graveyard shift — a twilight zone of pre-computer newspapering that existed nightly from midnight to eight. Half the editors who worked The Rim were drunks or incompetents, the other half recent arrivals (like David) or reporters who'd offended some middle manager (like Tolbert) and had to do penance.

They sat around long tables arranged in a U-shape, writing headlines by counting units and using fat pencils, pastepots and brushes to combine different wire-service versions of the same story. On The Rim work came in waves, and during quiet times, editors would kibbitz and argue. Often they'd draw on stories they found in *Le Devoir* or *The Chronicle*, early editions of which arrived around three in the morning.

David and Tolbert were the biggest talkers. They'd been bantering together since high school, when Tolbert immigrated from Trinidad, and could anticipate each other's moves.

"Did you see that item on page three?" David said on this particular night, while flipping through *The Chronicle*. "The language police hounding that poor old undertaker?"

"Don't you understand, mon?" Tolbert wasn't above using dialect for effect. "English signs blemish the French face of Montreal. Bill 101's a magic face cream. Got unsightly Anglos you want to get rid of? Try 101! Presto, they're gone!"

David sighed, said: "English is the *lingua franca* of the western world. I wish our Francophone colleagues would wake up to that."

"David, David. Middle-class Francophones have always been bilingual. They send their kids to private schools to make sure they stay that way."

"Your point, *Monsieur Tolbaire.*"

Usually this French mispronunciation would elicit a snappy retort, but Tolbert was on a roll: "The Quiet Revolution won't be finished until working-class Francophones realize how their middle-class leaders preserve their own privileges. And that's by keeping the underclass in unilingual isolation."

From the far end of the rim, an editor named Stanton observed: "We've got a Marxist in our midst."

"Quebec is an island," David said. "Francophones feel threatened."

"What about the small nations of Europe?" Stanton said. "The Dutch, the Norwegians, the Greeks. They pride themselves on speaking four or five languages."

"They're not surrounded," David said, "by an English-speaking sea."

Tolbert said: "This 'threatened' argument's just a smokescreen for xenophobia. Believe me, mon, I know racism when I see it."

"Have you read that book I lent you?"

"White Niggers of America? In this emerging nation, David, Anglophones are the only niggers. Anglophones white or black."

Stanton said: "Run that past me again?"

"Let's just agree," David said, "that all Quebecers, French or English, black or pink, could use a little consciousness-raising."

"Consciousness-raising? Ha! Back home, that's how my brother got into bookselling."

From Stanton: "We all know where that led."

"Wait, I see it now," David said, painting a sign in the air. "David Nelligan and Associates. Canadian and Caribbean Books."

"That's not bad," Tolbert said. "But try Tolbert and Company. And not just Caribbean, but First Nations, too. Universalize the struggle. Canadian, Caribbean and First Nations Books."

"Call the place Longhouse," David said. "Or, no, there's a Longhouse in Toronto. Wait, I've got it." Again he painted a sign in the air: "Calypso Canada Books."

Tolbert said: "I don't get it."

"Inclusiveness?" David said. "Topicality? Political dimension?"

Stanton said: "Calypso — the Greek goddess?"

"Not a goddess, an immortal," David said. "Forget Greek. Think Caribbean."

"Calypso Canada Books," Tolbert said. "You know, that's not bad."

7 / A BAFFLING APOLOGY

In the autumn of 1974, about his infatuation with Isabelle Garneau, David Nelligan resolved to do nothing. Part of him knew that his enchantment was a naive reaction to achievement in his chosen field. Besides, for the past five years he'd been faithful to Arianna and he'd vowed to remain that way. True, he'd patted a bottom or two and peeked down the occasional blouse. But that was it. And if, before marrying Arianna, he'd had escapades, he'd put all that behind him.

Isabelle lent him more of her novels. One she'd set in Outremont, the wealthy Montreal neighborhood in which she'd grown up; another in Paris, where she'd done graduate work at the Sorbonne; and a third in Mexico, where she'd lived for two years with her Swiss husband, a linguistics professor.

In those novels, David realized now, on Old Orchard Avenue, Isabelle revealed her psychological problems. In *Le Malin*, for example, her heroine committed suicide. And the narrator of *Visions à Minuit* was double-voiced, a split personality — both hunter and victim.

Wiser men understood and kept their distance.

But David delighted in Isabelle's pyrotechnics, and never mind the awkward subtext: Anglophobic, anti-male. At the Rymark Tavern he listened, entranced, while she told her story.

Isabelle's ex-husband, Kurt, had departed eighteen months before and gained custody of their two sons, sixteen and nine. She and Kurt owned a two-storey house in Outremont, and Isabelle lived there now — shared the place with a history professor, his wife and two children. She and Kurt also owned a cabin in the Laurentians, a weekend retreat near Ste-Adele.

To David at twenty-six, her life sounded, if not glorious, then certainly tangled, so rich and complex. He and Arianna had travelled across Canada and visited England and France — but on a shoestring. Now they were students again, scraping along in the McGill Ghetto in what Isabelle would later describe as "that dinky little apartment" on Aylmer Street.

Fair enough, David supposed now. Though both he and Arianna, having recently survived a cockroach-infested walk-up in Toronto's Cabbagetown, found the place convenient, affordable, blissfully clean.

Never mind. David was enchanted. Isabelle was so sophisticated, so experienced — so beautifully French in a worn way. She reminded him of the actress Jeanne Moreau. And at the Rymark, after a couple of beers, David would feel his resolve weaken. While making a point, he'd place his hand on Isabelle's thigh and she'd pretend not to notice.

One Friday, after two or three beers, Isabelle mentioned a casual boyfriend: maybe David had heard of Jacques Bienvenue? He ran a local publishing house, Editions Dufort: "Not bad for a twenty-eight-old, *quoi?*"

Oh, but their relationship wasn't serious. Mainly, she said, it was sexual: *"Avec lui, c'est du sexe, puis c'est tout."*

David had been trying not to think about having sex with Isabelle, kept telling himself she wouldn't be interested. She was forty years old, after all. And so accomplished. What did he have to offer? Still, she slept with Jacques Bienvenue. Why not him?

No, no. Impossible. What about Arianna?

The following Friday, again at the Rymark, Isabelle told him she was looking forward to getting away from her own house for the weekend. An old friend named Philippe Lachapelle, a translator, was travelling to New York for a conference and had asked her to care for his tropical fish. He lived in a semi-detached house on Rue Jeanne Mance, Isabelle said. There, away from the ringing phones and tumult of her communal home, she'd get some serious writing done. "It's just around the corner from you, David." She mentioned the address. "Why don't you visit?"

Earlier, despite his resolve, David had asked plaintively, half-joking: "Will we never be alone together?" But he hadn't expected Isabelle to call his bluff. Surprised, he began waffling, mumbling about a non-existent commitment. From across the table, T.J. asked, "What are you two whispering about?"

This he said almost belligerently, though David attributed his tone to rough edges. T.J. not only hailed from northern Ontario but was older, early thirties, and tough-looking. Claimed he'd been a golden-gloves boxer.

Pronouncing his name the French way, but speaking in English, Isabelle said brightly: "*Monsieur Nelligan* here wants to know when I'm going to sleep with him."

The silence didn't last forever. But to David it felt that way. Finally Tolbert, who didn't attend the novel-writing workshop but frequently joined the party afterwards, took pity on him: "Send that naughty boy to the end of the line."

Everybody laughed and resumed talking.

Everybody but David. He sat stunned, grateful for the relative darkness of the tavern. Isabelle had deliberately embarrassed him. But why? They didn't speak again that afternoon — everybody was watching — and parted on *Rue Ste-Catherine* with a casual wave.

A cold rain had begun falling. Still reeling, not wanting to talk, David declined Tolbert's offer of a lift and walked home through the rush-hour crowd, seeing nothing.

Arianna was already home. He kissed her on the cheek, then went into the kitchen-nook and began making spaghetti while she talked about her latest design project, an apartment block, and also a woman friend who thought she was pregnant. This was his life.

Except that Isabelle had invited him to visit — and alone. To do what came naturally? That she'd implied. But then, in front of half the workshop, she'd humiliated him. Why? Because he'd hesitated? David had to sort this out.

That, at least, is what he told himself.

He told Arianna, after supper, that he needed to visit the libarary, do some research. She offered to join him, but he said he wanted to walk alone in the rain and gather impressions for his novel. No problem. Arianna had plenty to do.

At eight o'clock, sheltering under a big black umbrella, David mounted the steps of a semi-detached house on Jeanne Mance and pressed the buzzer.

What happened next, David knew, Isabelle had described, in *Le Diable Entre Nous,* better than he ever would. Though with a vindictive twist. Himself sitting on the couch in too-short blue jeans, an earnest L'il Abner. His umbrella open on the floor beside him, drying, looking like a giant raven.

Isabelle wore a low-cut peasant blouse and a floor-length skirt, South American. Her thick black hair, her best feature, tumbled to her bare shoulders. Why had she done what she did, David wanted to know. Why had she deliberately humiliated him?

Isabelle sat down beside him on the couch. She stroked his hand, said the remark had just popped out and she was sorry. "I don't play games," she said. "You and I could never have a casual affair, David. We're both too serious."

"You're right," he said. He was having trouble breathing. "We'd better give this business a rest."

He extricated his hand, excused himself, walked down the hall to the bathroom. There he splashed cold water in his face, stood staring into the mirror. He thought of Arianna and decided to leave. He'd return to the living room, say goodbye and walk out the door.

But he had only one gesture left. That he knew. If Isabelle tried to stop him, he wouldn't be strong enough to leave.

Back in the living room, David picked up his jacket: "I'd better be on my way."

"Oh, but you haven't seen the tropical fish," Isabelle said in French. "Don't you want to see the fish?"

Without looking back, she walked away down the hall.

David's mouth went dry. He dropped his jacket on the couch and followed Isabelle into a guest bedroom. Three fish tanks bubbled madly. Isabelle bent over and pointed: "Look at those lovely striped guys."

Her voice was thick.

David put his hands on her shoulders. She turned and came into his arms. Together they fell onto the bed.

For five years, David had made love with nobody but Arianna. Now Isabelle Garneau, brilliant Québécoise novelist, lay beneath him with her legs spread, moaning his name.

David went wild.

Two hours later, when, fully clothed, he stood hugging Isabelle goodbye, she said: "I have a feeling I should say I'm sorry."

"Sorry? Sorry for what?"
Isabelle patted his cheek.

8 / STILL A BOY AT TWENTY-SIX

Why had it taken English Quebec so long to wake up to its peril? Why, in the beginning, hadn't he read between the lines of Isabelle's novels? Naiveté and arrogance, both cases. So David Nelligan told himself, pacing around the house in 1989. Just as well-meaning Anglos had sought to accomodate draconian language laws — though every court in the land declared Bill 101 discriminatory and unconstitutional — so with Isabelle he'd insisted on playing by old-fashioned rules.

He'd grown up far from the bright lights of the city, and it was as if, when he met Isabelle, he was in his early and not his middle twenties. Hopelessly romantic, he'd decided they could share a clandestine love affair, rely on discretion and mutual respect.If he'd been a better reader, he thought now, more alert to precedents, analogies and implications, he wouldn't have been so shocked, later, at Isabelle's vindictiveness.

Now, David realized that his painful innocence stood forth in what he did immediately after making love to Isabelle for the first time. He walked into the "dinky little apartment" he called home and, in response to Arianna's worried query about where he'd been, blurted: "I can't lie to you, Arianna. I've just slept with Isabelle."

Still a boy at twenty-six.

Hard to face, this. But for five, six years, he and Arianna had shared everything. They'd built no privacies into their relationship, kept no secrets. Oh, he'd been able to say, the Friday before, that at the Rymark he'd talked mostly with Tolbert when in fact he'd done nothing but listen to Isabelle.

But greater falsity than that he could not yet contain. Making love with Isabelle — his first Other Woman — had been momentous, overwhelming, an experience far larger than he'd expected.

"You slept with Isabelle? What are you saying?"

"Arianna, I —"

"No! Get away! Don't touch me!"

Arianna disappeared into their bedroom. David sat at the kitchen table staring into space, listening to her weep. Twice he knocked on the door. The first time, she yelled at him to go away. The second, she jerked open the door and threw blankets in his face.

Through the door, David said: "Arianna, I'm sorry. It just happened."

"Go take a shower. You stink!"

"I already took a shower."

"You still stink. Take another one."

David showered again but Arianna refused to open the bedroom door. That night he slept, badly, on the couch. Next morning, from a phone booth, he called Isabelle and told her he'd confessed.

"You what?"

"I told Arianna what happened."

"I don't believe this."

"Isabelle, we can't let it happen again."

"What?"

"It! It! We can't let it happen again."

"You're right, David. You're right. But now I feel badly. We should get together and talk, the three of us."

"Isabelle, I don't think that's a good idea."

"There's no reason we can't remain friends, David. Besides, we've got to resolve the house business."

David and Arianna had been talking with Isabelle about living communally next term, moving into her house in Outremont. The history professor and his wife were moving out and Isabelle needed help with the mortgage.

"I don't know, Isabelle. I don't think Arianna —"

"David, we've got to talk about this."

Arianna didn't want to see Isabelle. And where before she'd been ready to consider moving into the elegant redbrick house in Outremont, she and David taking over the top floor, now she wanted no part of this. But Isabelle had insisted on visiting and, rather than make David call her back, Arianna said, "All right, let her come."

The following afternoon, Isabelle arrived early. David was still at Concordia, attending a lecture — as she'd known he would be — and the two women talked alone. Isabelle assured Arianna that she had no intention of breaking up anybody's marriage. Her ex-best friend had done that to her, Isabelle said, and she herself would be incapable of inflicting such pain on another woman. Besides, she was still in love with her ex-husband.

Having created an atmosphere of shared intimacies — that's how, bemused, Arianna later described it — Isabelle waited. And Arianna, fourteen years younger, said that David was starry-eyed when it came to published authors. That he believed fiction-writing was a vocation, and the published author stood at the right hand of God. "You could lure him away if you wanted," she said. "I wouldn't be able to stop you."

David arrived for the denouement. They were all sorry IT had happened. But they were all three adults. Life went on. Isabelle mentioned in passing that, if David and Arianna decided to share her Outremont house this fall, she'd let them use her cabin in Ste-Adele as well. A month or so earlier, they'd visited, travelling north by bus. They'd sprawled on the rug in front of the fireplace, drunk too much red wine and played Triple Yahtzee into the wee hours. Arianna had loved the cabin. But now she remained non-committal.

When Isabelle left, with kisses on both cheeks all round, Arianna said forget it. No way she was moving into the Outremont house. Not after what had happened. David relayed this, somewhat softened, and Isabelle said she was sorry to hear that. But, hey, they were all three adults. And now, once or twice a week, Isabelle would find herself in the neighborhood and drop in to chat with whomever was home.

One afternoon, finding David alone, she invited him to spend July in Ste-Adele with her and her sons, no strings attached. Arianna had enrolled for a summer course at the university, but why should he remain cooped up in the city? In Ste-Adele, he could sleep and work out back, in the writing shed. The perfect place to complete this latest draft of his novel.

David didn't say no. Though he knew perfectly well that Arianna would never go for this. Are you kidding? He also knew Montreal in July — nothing but heat and humidity. He imagined himself sweltering at a typewriter, compared this with a vision of floating on an air mattress in the middle of a Laurentian lake.

To Arianna, instead of mentioning Ste-Adele, he suggested that maybe they should, after all, move into Isabelle's house in Outremont. When she remained adamant, he told her: "You're too conventional. You're judging Isabelle by normal standards. You forget she's a writer."

Disgusted, Arianna picked up her staplegun and turned to her latest design project: "David, I've got work to do."

In 1989, as he paced around the house in west-end Montreal, remembering, David realized he hadn't yet come clean. The Outremont house, the cabin at the lake — yes, these exposed his crass materialism, and so reflected badly on him. This implied he was being honest.

But he'd downplayed the sex. Why? Lust had played a key role. He'd wanted Isabelle. And certainly she'd wanted him. You wouldn't know it to look at him now, shuffling around in baggy jeans and slippers, but in his mid-twenties, David Nelligan cut quite a figure. If he wasn't a black-haired Adonis, probably he was as close as Isabelle would ever come. And she knew it. Fact is, having made love once, both of them wanted desperately to do it again. Only difference was, David tried to smother this desire and Isabelle stoked it.

One night not long after Isabelle suggested the July sojourn, David and Arianna ran into her in the library at the *Université de Montréal*. Arianna was hunting a specific design book, and David and Isabelle found themselves alone in Québécois literature. Suddenly, she was in his arms. He was kissing her, touching her breasts.

They pulled apart, stunned.

That night, David wrote a note saying "no" to Ste-Adele. Began it: "Dear Queen Bee." Now, in west-end Montreal, he smiled grimly at his taste for melodrama. But then he wrote: "Six hours have elapsed since I kissed you in the stacks. Arianna has long since gone to bed. This business among us has reached an impasse. I'm on my fourth cup of coffee. Tolbert was right when he said I was in love with the idea of being in love with you. It's equally true that we don't NOT fit. But July in Ste-Adele would be both a beginning and an ending — anathema to the writer in me. I won't kiss you again in the stacks, Isabelle. But that doesn't mean I won't think about it."

This he signed, "Nobody's Drone."

In *Le Diable Entre Nous,* Isabelle wrote that she responded in the same vein, agreed they should stop seeing each other. But now David turned up the note she'd sent him. She'd been sitting at home with her friend Philippe Lachapelle, the translator who owned gold fish, talking about seizing the day, and how we only pass this way once, when the mail arrived. Now she sat curled up in her favorite armchair, shaking.

She'd been thinking of visiting him, of admitting that her morality was just a fear of getting hurt, so maybe they should all three just accept what was happening and see where it led. She was horribly sad about the Queen Bee reference. Didn't he understand that she'd been trying to distance herself? But she wasn't a castrating female, truly she wasn't.

David might be in love with the idea of being in love with her, as Tolbert suggested. But over the weekend she'd realized an awful truth about herself: She was in love with him. That didn't mean she couldn't handle it, or wouldn't get over it. But it was true. And she was tired of fighting it.

Now she was crying and crying and just feeling so alone. She did believe that you could love more than one person at a time. She did believe that. But never mind, David didn't. And he was the one who would have to do that kind of loving.

Isabelle handed him this letter at the Rymark Tavern after the novel-writing workshop. Next day, with Arianna well-launched into working on her design project, David said he was going downtown to visit bookstores. Instead, he rode the Number 80 bus up Park Avenue to Rue Laurier, then walked the tree-lined streets to Isabelle's house.

This time, when he arrived home at his "dinky little apartment" on Aylmer, he confessed nothing.

9 / TRUDGING IN DARKNESS

Still a boy at twenty-six? Nobody would even begin to understand, David realized, unless they knew about Ste-Thérèse-sur-le-lac. Creating a political allegory would mean writing about his boyhood — about delivering newspapers and losing the rent money and struggling to bridge the two so-called solitudes. Now, though, on Old Orchard Avenue, David stood surveying the disordered jumble he'd made of the living room.

He'd sorted the contents of his cardboard boxes, stacked letters and notebooks and file folders everywhere but beside his desk, where he'd dumped his law books. In one of the boxes, he'd discovered a forgotten set of bongo drums. He'd brought them back from Africa, hadn't played them in years. On impulse, David picked his way across the room and retrieved these bongos. Then he sat down, wedged them between his knees and began tapping away, thinking about Ste-Thérèse.

For the first time, last week's impromptu visit made sense — began to look almost synchronistic. He'd woken up, looked out the window and decided that he'd read one too many law books. For eight or nine days he'd been wrestling with the niceties of arson and libel law. Outside, the winter day sparkled. Surely he'd earned a break?

Quickly, before he could change his mind, David dressed and ate breakfast. Then he climbed into his rattletrap Chevy and, without consciously settling on any destination, drove north along Decarie Boulevard. He swung onto the Laurentian autoroute and that's when he realized where, via expressway, he was heading — to Ste-Thérèse-sur-le-lac.

Back when he was growing up, in the nineteen fifties and sixties, to reach Ste-Thérèse by car you drove north out of Montreal across the Cartierville Bridge, then followed a twisting two-lane highway through a series of small towns. At St-Eustache you crossed a second, smaller bridge, then meandered west along the Lac des Deux- Montagnes through Bonaventure to the village of Ste-Thérèse.

David hadn't visited for eight or nine years, and as he drove pensively into town — what was he doing here anyway? — he registered the place against the backdrop of boyhood. Gone was the old black train bridge that had marked the centre of town. And where once train tracks ran away into the distance both ways, disappearing into forest, now a paved bicycle path curved along a ridge and over-looked manicured lawns.

The hotel, *La Fin du Monde,* remained where it belonged. Likewise the gas station, Esso, and the grocery store, Marché Champroux. But the *Salle de Danse,* which once attracted teenagers from all over the North Shore, had been replaced by a redbrick town hall. For grandeur, this *hotel de ville* rivalled the French Roman Catholic Church that lay up the highway to the west.

Opposite the town hall stood a funeral parlour, *Laflamme et Fils.* And kitty corner across the highway, where in boyhood he'd caught tadpoles with Emmanuel Tolbert, a strip mall had erupted out of the earth. A *dépanneur,* a video outlet, a laundromat, a bicycle repair shop — in new-look Ste-Thérèse, you could play miniature golf, rent a mobile home, even phone for a pizza.

The town he grew up in no longer existed.

David drove slowly up and down snow-packed streets, searching among refurbished bungalows and three-storey mansions for shacks and chalets that survived from his youth. He delighted in recognizing these places, some of them completely redone, others untouched — and especially the houses of former paper-route customers. There, that was the Casgrain place, three knock-out teenage girls who hadn't known he existed; and there stood the renovated home of *Monsieur Talibert,* a summer customer who, come Labor Day, would always tip him with a five-dollar bill.

Rolling slowly along, peering through the windshield at a town both strange and familiar, David imagined that he could see through the movie-set suburb before him to the town he'd known as a boy, when in summer, because of its sandy beach, Ste-Thérèse became a poor-man's resort. Its population exploded into the thousands and on Friday nights a loud-speaker truck would roll up and down the streets blaring: *"Attention s'il vous plait, attention. Grand bingo demain soir à sept heures à l'église Ste-Thérèse. Mille dollars de prix à gagner. Demain soir à l'église Ste-Thérèse. Bingo!"*

For most of the year, though, Ste-Thérèse was home to maybe five hundred souls, among them a few Anglais. Streets were dirt roads, hard-packed, most of them running south from the highway to the lake: *Avenue des Anges, Avenue des Archanges, Avenue des Oracles.* And houses were rickety, clapboard affairs on stilts, uninsulated summer camps raised high off the ground because of the threat of spring flooding.

Now, as David drove these empty, snow-banked streets, he thought of his newspaper route and wondered whether his bloody-minded intransigence, as Arianna called it, didn't derive from his years of trudging around in early-morning darkness. Maybe that was what he'd been sent here to learn? That he owed his resolve and determination, his tenacity and sense of purpose, to his long-ago experience as a paper boy?

Together with the newspaper route came images of his mother. She'd shared this year-long endurance test, he realized — this marathon that he'd begun at age nine and was still running five years later, rising in darkness six days a week, fifty-two weeks a year, every year of his early adolescence.

Now that he thought about it, navigating the icy streets at a crawl, picking out original houses, David understood that, at the outset, at least, the resolve and determination had been his mother's. And it was as if, by example — and though sometimes she urged him to quit — she'd deliberately recreated those traits in him.

Back came the most vivid dream of his boyhood, then, the one that began with himself exclaiming, "Look, Madame Binette!" while pulling twenty-dollar bills out of his pocket and flinging them into the air. "Look! The rent money's nothing! How much do we owe you?"

"David, it's time." His mother's voice.

"No, no." The best was yet to come. Out of another pocket he pulled a wad of bills and started peeling off hundreds, counting them aloud, one and two and three and....

"Twenty past five, love."

... and it was just his mother, shaking him awake, whispering so as not to wake his brother in the bunk above him: "Time to do the papers."

"Okay, I'm awake."

His mother left the curtain open so he wouldn't fall back to sleep. From the kitchen came the sound of the radio, the announcer saying it was thirty degrees below zero, more like forty below if you considered the wind. David listened while the man ran down the names of schools that had already closed because of the weather.

He kicked off the covers and, still without opening his eyes, threw his feet over the side of the bed. Freezing cold, the floor. David grabbed his socks from under the bed and pulled them on, tucked in his pajama bottoms.

"Half past five, David," his mother called from the kitchen. "Better get a move on."

"Okay, I'm coming." It was cold enough that he could see his breath.

In the top bunk, Eddie rolled over and said, "Not so loud, eh?"

David pulled his jeans over his pajamas and stood up, careful not to bang his head on the top bunk. He scooped up the rest of his clothes and, shivering, trotted out into the kitchen to finish dressing by the oil stove.

His mother was hunched over the table in her old bathrobe, making lunches. The blue-and-white *Chronicle* bag hung empty on the arm chair beside her. Before waking him, his mother always pulled a coat over her bathrobe, stepped out the back door and retrieved the newspapers from the bottom of the stairs. She'd cut the wire around the bundle, fold the papers and stuff them, one by one, into the bag.

He pulled on a third sweater: "No papers?"

"Not by the steps. It's snowing pretty bad."

"Damn."

His mother glanced up but said nothing. David pulled on his old grey duffle coat and did up the buttons. Then he buckled on his boots and kicked the rug away from in front of the door. His mother handed him the flashlight. "You should quit this job," she said. "It's crazy, going out in a storm like this. You could earn enough spending money doing odd jobs for *Monsieur Therrien.*"

David grunted. Then out he went, pulling the door shut behind him. Blowing snow stung his eyes. The steps were icy, treacherous, and as he descended he held onto the rickety wooden railing his father had built the summer before. Enough light streamed through the window over the kitchen sink that he could see clearly around the bottom of the stairs. The newspapers weren't there.

David flicked on the flashlight and made his way down the edge of the driveway, kicking at the drifted snow. He was so bundled up in sweaters and scarves that, except for his face, he didn't feel the cold. But the wind was fierce and on the highway, he knew, the blowing snow would become a million stinging pinpricks.

Looked like the truck driver hadn't made it down the street. Was he a new guy or what? David would have to retrieve the wire cutters from inside the house, then fight his way up *Avenue des Oracles* to check in front of the hotel. Maybe, because of the storm, the driver had been able to get that far and no farther. If the newspapers were there, fine. He'd do the whole route backwards, begin delivering at Mrs. Johannson's, up along the train tracks beyond the grocery store.

If they weren't, he'd return home empty-handed. His mother would phone the circulation office and get them to send more papers from Bonaventure. That second batch wouldn't arrive until noon. If school were cancelled, no problem. Away he'd go. Other-wise, his mother would get dressed and deliver *The Chronicles* herself, hauling the baby on the toboggan.

David had almost abandoned the search when, at the base of his brother's snow fort, he spotted an odd pile of snow. The papers! The truck driver must have flung the bundle out the door, pulled a U-turn and taken off.

Back in the house, David waited on the rug while his mother cut the wire that bound the newspapers. "School cancelled?"

"Not yet." She folded each paper and stuffed it into the blue-and-white bag all in one motion. He enjoyed watching her do this — her efficiency. "I think they mentioned Our Lady of the Roses."

"What's the Protestant Board trying to prove?"

All English-speaking children from Ste-Thérèse went to school in Bonaventure: Roman Catholics to Our Lady of the Roses, Protestants to Lake Bonaventure High. This last, despite its name, accommodated grades one to eleven. Every school day, together with two or three other kids, David would wait on the highway in front of the hotel for the station wagon — more recently, a yellow school bus — that left from Oka, collected children along the way and drove them all to Bonaventure.

"At least you don't have basketball practice," his mother said.

"I still think they should cancel," David said — though he realized, with relief, that she was right. Practices were Tuesday and Thursday, starting at eight, one hour before classes. As the youngest guy on the junior boys' team, and the only seventh grader, he never missed a practice. He'd deliver his newspapers and then, instead of returning to bed for an hour, eat breakfast and hitchhike into Bonaventure.

But today was Wednesday and, if school went ahead, he'd catch the bus in front of the hotel with the other English kids. Wouldn't have to worry about not getting a ride, like on the morning that kept coming back. Usually he'd get a lift right away and be standing at the front door of the school, flapping his arms, when the janitor arrived. If he didn't get picked up within fifteen minutes, he'd start walking, hitching as he went.

That particular morning, he'd had to walk all the way to school, more than two miles, and so arrived late for basketball practice. He changed quickly and ran down the hall to the gym just in time for scrimmage. Not until second period, scripture, did he remember the rent money.

Now he slung the *Chronicle* bag over his shoulder: "Ten here?"

"Yes, I counted twice." His mother opened the door for him. "I still think you should quit this job."

"Mother, please," he said. But as he descended the treacherous back steps for the second time that morning, David wondered. Some days, even in winter, he enjoyed delivering *Chronicles*. Last Friday, with the snow on the street hard-packed as ice, and still no sign of the sand truck, he'd laced on his skates and away he'd flown, pretending he was Rocket Richard. Cut delivery time in half.

Today he wasn't enjoying. The cold, the dark — these were as always. But snow was slicing down in sheets, blown by the wind. At the end of the driveway David turned right, happy that, to begin, at least, he had the wind at his back.

All his winter customers but one lived, like the Nelligans, on *Avenue des Oracles*. First he'd go down the street towards the lake: Arsenault, Callaghan, Boyd, Therrien and Old Pelletier. Then he'd march back up, glimpsing his mother through their front window, hunched over the kitchen table, making his father's breakfast. Belanger, Middleton, Morrissette, Talbot. Finally, he'd swing up the highway past the grocery store, Marché Champroux, and along the train tracks to Mrs. Johannson's.

David moved to the middle of the street and shut his eyes. He'd open them only when the crunch of the snow beneath his feet told him he'd wandered. This way, he found, he could dream while he worked. Once or twice, he'd awoken outside Mrs. Johannson's with a left-over newspaper in his bag, wondering if his mother had miscounted (unlikely), or if he'd missed somebody. And praying it wasn't *Monsieur Morrissette.*

Crunch, crunch, crunch. The snow was getting deeper. David opened one eye just enough to change direction. If he could hang on for a few more months, summer would arrive. Ste-Thérèse was a resort town, and come July, with the influx of vacationers, his paper route would explode. He'd have thirty-five or forty customers, all within two miles of the house.

He'd ride his old bicycle, pedal like crazy, see how quickly he could deliver. The sun would come up while he worked. If he wasn't going to set a record, he'd stop a moment by the lake, down by Old Pelletier's, watch the haze lift off the water. Barring a flat tire or trouble with the chain, he'd be finished inside three quarters of an hour and back in bed by six fifteen. With tips, he'd clear five or six dollars a week — a small fortune.

Callaghan's was dark. David mounted the steps, opened the outside door and knocked on the one inside. Down the hall a light went on. He deposited the *Chronicle* between the doors and headed back onto the street. The summer people returned to Montreal after Labor Day, and overnight his route shrank to ten or twelve papers. Still, along with the small-route subsidy, he'd make two or three dollars a week — enough to keep him independent. And it was steady, not like the odd jobs his mother found him. In autumn, he could still ride his bicycle, and delivering took eighteen or twenty minutes.

The trouble with autumn was the rain. Once or twice a week his mother would fetch the papers and half of them would be soaked. They'd have to decide, then, who was going to get a wet newspaper. They tried to alternate victims but *Monsieur Morrissette,* for one, could never be given a wet newspaper because when Saturday rolled around, collection day, he'd refuse to pay for it. David would have to make up the difference himself — and again he thought of the rent money.

That's what they called it, rent money, though really it was payments on the house. Once a month after school, David had to deliver this rent money, trudging twenty minutes along the highway from the school to *Madame Binette's* house in St-Eustache. He hated this chore. He didn't mind missing the school bus and having to hitchhike home. And *Madame Binette* he liked. She'd invite him inside, offer him milk and cookies.

No, what he hated was being given a receipt for May's rent money in October, or for last November's in July. And *Madame Binette,* honestly confused, flipping through her records, saying, *"C'est correct, ca?"* And David having to say, *"Oui, c'est correct."*

So always he'd put the rent money out of his mind until it came time to deliver. Again that terrible morning came back, second period, when David realized that in his rush to reach the gym for basketball practice, he'd neglected to lock his locker. He decided to check, just to be sure. The teacher was droning on about loaves and fishes.

Under his desk, David opened his wallet — and found it empty. The classroom began to spin. David turned his wallet this way and that, disbelieving, then stumbled to his feet and bolted for the door.

The teacher, startled, jumped out of the way. " David?"

"Got to see the principal."

He raced down the hall, took the steps two at a time, and didn't stop running until he reached the principal's office.

"Mr. Noble!" He banged on the door. "Mr. Noble, I've been robbed!"

10 / DAMAGE REPORT

At five o'clock, David Nelligan set aside his rediscovered bongos. He stood up, drew back the curtain and blew another hole in the ice. Already it was pitch dark outside. Beneath a street lamp, the three would-be party-goers were still struggling to free their van, rocking it back and forth. Two of them, he realized now, were women — though he couldn't have said how he knew.

David let the curtain fall and resumed his seat. Glanced down at the pile of law books beside his desk. Arson, libel and slander. Almost an expert, he'd become, driven to it by political attack. Or no: make that ideological.

Here he spotted a parallel: the nationalism of *La Nouvelle* and the feminism of Isabelle Garneau. Both were cover stories for vindictiveness.

He picked up *Le Diable Entre Nous*. Amazing, the way Isabelle had rewritten the truth to serve her own ends. Though she'd also contrived to create "herstory" as she went along, so later she'd merely have to report it. Hence the relentlessness he'd felt, that sense of being trapped in the undertow of someone else's quest.

David remembered discovering *Le Diable*. What, ten years before? Summer, 1979. *The Montreal Standard* was back in business after the pressmen's strike. During the work stoppage, numerous staffers had taken Highway 401 to Toronto and points west. As a result, and with Tolbert's backing, he'd got back onto the street as a general reporter. Late one morning, while swinging down *Rue St-Denis* after interviewing a movie mogul, he ducked into a French-language bookstore to browse.

At first he didn't realize what he'd picked up. He was checking out a variety of new titles and the process of identification ran something like: trade paperback, literary press, buff cover, title in red: *Le Diable Entre Nous. Un roman.* Isabelle Garneau. My God! The threatened novel!

David bought the book. Outside, he decided against heading for the cafés and bistros of Old Montreal, where he'd undoubtedly run into friends and colleagues. Instead, he made for a greasy spoon on

The Main. There, for the first time, over a toasted bacon-and-tomato sandwich, David read Isabelle's novel. Not closely, but closely enough to see that it was far more savage and damning than he'd dreamed possible. He had a flash of Isabelle standing in the hallway, red-cheeked and furious, her voice icy cold: "You'll pay for this, David Nelligan. You'll pay for this."

Isabelle had turned him into a sexual predator: a rake and a rambling boy, too good-looking by half. He was a Svengali figure, a deceitful sorcerer who'd say or do anything to get into a woman's pants. Herself she'd styled a woman alone, recently deserted by her husband, vulnerable to the blandishments, despite her best intentions, of this dispicable, two-timing cad.

On Old Orchard, David growled and shook his head. Ten years, he'd had, to digest this vile work — and still it enfuriated him. Of course he'd wanted to take Isabelle to bed. He'd thought he was in love and no further. Isabelle saw beyond the bedroom — though only the most careful reader would recognize that. Never mind that she'd been forty, and then forty-one to his twenty-six. In her novel she'd slashed the difference to eight years. She gave herself away by rhapsodizing about his athlete's body, his mane of wild black hair — but how many would see that?

And Arianna? Isabelle had turned her into a mindless nonentity. No sensitivity, no sense of humor, no passion for art and adventure. True, Isabelle did allow that her rival was drop-dead gorgeous: large brown eyes, red hair that tumbled halfway down her back, thick and wavy. A trim, athletic figure. Svelte, in fact. But this she condoned only because it reflected well on her own attractiveness. And it wasn't fair, you see? Why should this spoiled Canadian bitch have everything, including a man? And our aggrieved *Québécoise* nothing?

Reading all this, skimming it really, in that greasy spoon on The Main, David could hardly believe his eyes. Malicious? Isabelle had betrayed every tender moment. He'd allowed himself to be vulnerable and now, in this vicious *roman à clef,* she was trying to humiliate him. No, to destroy him. Such vehemence! Isabelle revealed that at times she wanted to murder him, to drive a stake through his evil heart, then slice him into tiny pieces. Naked, unmitigated hatred, this — and so utterly self-serving. He reeled to think that Isabelle

Garneau, celebrated for the emotional honesty of her work, could write and publish a work so false.

Now, at his desk, David smiled grimly at this first reaction. How young he'd been, even a decade ago. He'd known Isabelle was writing a novel about him. She'd warned him at Black Water Books. They hadn't seen each other alone, though they'd run into each other a couple of times, since she'd exploded at the news of Arianna's pregnancy. Then this one Saturday, after the usual pleasantries, Isabelle had said she was finishing a novel about them — and probably he wouldn't like it.

He'd shrugged: *"Alors, c'est la guerre?"*

She'd smiled and said nothing.

Still, unprepared. Same with Arianna. Initially, knowing it would hurt her, he delayed showing her the novel. He put it off for days, until finally she confronted him, demanded to know why he was so depressed and cranky and walking around with that hangdog look on his face.

All through her pregnancy, even knowing how she'd reacted to the fact of it, Arianna had treated Isabelle with civility. Not like the year before, when they'd all three tried to maintain friendly relations, but with great *politesse*.

Now, boom: *Le Diable Entre Nous.*

"She pretended to be my friend," Arianna said, stunned. "Then she turned me into this milquetoast — this bimbo."

"The novel's meant to hurt us. That's what it's designed to do."

"The woman is sick! Remember how she behaved in Greece? Her rages and tantrums? None of that appears in the novel."

"No demons, no suicide threats."

"I believed she was sincere — that she really was trying to be friends. What a fool I was. She was just milking me for information."

"I didn't expect such hatred."

"She hated you before she met you, David. You're male, you're English."

"I'm not English, I'm Canadian! I'm part-French and part-Irish and part-Mohawk and —"

"To Isabelle you're English, David. *Voila, c'est tout.*"

Later, for Emmanuel Tolbert, David described the novel as equal parts venom, vitriol and vindictiveness.

"Don't keep it all inside, mon. Tell me how you really feel."

"Isabelle made no attempt to fictionalize, to cover her tracks. She went out of her way to pillory me."

"From what you've told me, she's always worked from life."

"She's trying to destroy me, Tolbert."

"So the hero's a male chauvinist, so what?"

"He's a loudmouth Canadian pig — a jealous 'little man' who can't make the grade. Can't meet the challenge of becoming equal partners with a liberated *Québécoise,* and so goes scurrying back to his wife, an insipid little Ontarian."

"The novel's political?"

"That's what I'm trying to tell you!"

Tolbert never did read *Le Diable Entre Nous.* Didn't have the French for it. And David could never bring himself to tell the whole truth.

A liar, a hypocrite, an emotional coward — these charges, eventually, he could have laughed off. But Isabelle had also portrayed him as a talentless poseur. She'd never taken him seriously as a writer, she wrote, and nobody of substance ever would.

She'd known him well enough to wound him deeply — he had to give her that. Even now he had trouble acknowledging the extent of the damage. Before her novel appeared, all through the pressmen's strike, he'd worked steadily, revising the novel he'd drafted in Greece. When he returned to *The Standard,* he began rising at five in the morning to continue this work.

Then came *Le Diable Entre Nous* — the Bill 101 of his private life. And though David admitted it to nobody — not to Tolbert, not to Arianna, not even to himself — Isabelle's novel accomplished on a personal level what the language law had set out to do on a collective one. It silenced him. After Le Diable, David could still punch out journalism on demand. But fiction he could no longer write.

11 / TRAVELLING
WITH ONE OF THE IMMORTALS

Maybe I should have started further back — not with Greece but with the Norwegian freighter that brought us there. I think of our last night on that ship, the Evanger, when I stood alone on deck gazing up at a million stars, the sea calm, the night silent except for the distant churning of engines.

Isabelle joined me from below. She stood leaning against the wooden railing, her black hair blowing, and said she'd been re-reading *The Odyssey*. "Do you remember Calypso?"

"Some goddess, no?"

"One of the immortals. Odysseus was shipwrecked and ended up on her island. Calypso fell in love with him and refused to let him leave."

"I remember now. The gods were angry with him."

Isabelle nodded. "Imagine poor Odysseus pining for his wife, the tears streaming down his cheeks. For seven years, Calypso keeps him prisoner. Finally the gods tell her, enough: time to let him go. She knows better than to disobey. At first Odysseus won't believe her, that she's really offering to set him free. Calypso makes him a final offer: If he'll stay with her, she'll grant him immortality and ageless youth."

Isabelle paused for effect, then added: "Graciously, he declines. 'You're an immortal,' he says, 'and my wife is only human — but I want to return to Ithaca.'"

"Alors, Isabelle. Calypso, c'est toi?"

Isabelle grinned: "They celebrate before he leaves. Calypso eats ambrosia, food of the gods. To Odysseus she gives 'food fit for mortals.'" I could hear the quotation marks. "Don't you just love that?"

No, I'm rusty. I should have evoked that scene in flashback, and begun my story the following day, with our arrival at Pireaus. We'd lived on the freighter for a week and a half, used it as a floating hotel while visiting the Canary Islands, Genoa and Naples, Barcelona and Limossol, and I remember the shock of debarking, the suddenness of rejoining the real world as we climbed down fly-away stairs into a boat launch.

Waving goodbye to the junior officers, I felt both guilty and jubilant. I was five hundred dollars richer than when I'd embarked.

This after the other passengers, seven or eight retirees, had warned me not to play poker with sailors. Isabelle had staked me fifty dollars and with her I'd split my winnings — five hundred each.

Now, grandly, I hailed a taxi. We crammed our bags into the back seat, piled Isabelle's trunk and wicker hampers on top and rode to the ferry dock. There we bought tickets for that night's ferry, splurging on a private cabin. We left our gear at the office and rode a crowded bus into Athens, nothing but traffic and dust and honking horns.

At the American Express office, we both collected plenty of mail — but the bonanza was mine: half a dozen fat letters from Arianna in Africa.

I knew better than to tear them open on the spot.

We sat drinking wine at one of the outdoor cafés in Syntagma Square. Tourists scurried in and out of the airlines offices that ringed the square and Greek lotharios worked the tables, trying to pick up visiting women. Isabelle began to worry that we might miss the ferry. Neither of us was anxious to ride another overcrowded bus, and so we returned to Piraeus by taxi.

I paid to have our gear brought onto the ferry, then found myself striding along, empty-handed, appalled, while an old man hauled Isabelle's trunk on a cart, working like a dray horse. Earlier, on the freighter, advised by the poker-playing junior officers, I'd bought two cartons of American cigarettes. Now, our gear safely stowed, I gave the old man six packs.

I ached to read my letters from Arianna. But I waited until we'd settled into our cramped cabin. I waited, wanting to read alone, thinking Isabelle would realize this and, out of politeness, go for a stroll. She'd mentioned wanting to go for a walk. But no. She settled down on her bunk with a novel and I knew that if I went up on deck, she'd want to come. Finally, unable to wait any longer, I picked up my letters, slipped into the bathroom and began to read.

Arianna! I forgot everything but Arianna.

After a few moments, Isabelle said she was heading up on deck. I said fine, see you later, and took to my bunk. Arianna wrote of arriving in Wajadili — the stifling heat and humidity, the vegetation, the color. She described the project she was helping design. She enclosed sketches. She wrote of missing me. I finished the letters and lay dreaming of Arianna as long as I dared. Then went up on deck and found Isabelle.

We'd decided to eat dinner in the first-class dining room, one last splurge, and away we went, Isabelle chattering happily. The usual warning signs were there — the high-pitched voice, the nervous prattle — but I failed to notice. We ordered lamb souvla and, while waiting, polished off a half-litre of Greek wine. Isabelle called for a second bottle. After all, we were celebrating: "To Greece and Wajadili!" she said. "Especially to Wajadili, where one of us has already gone."

At that I woke up.

But before I could respond, the steward appeared and asked if he could seat another couple at our table. The dining room was over-crowded and he wasn't really asking. The man was Belgian, the woman Dutch. They looked older than me, younger than Isabelle. Resided in Paris, spoke beautiful French. Professionals. Very civilized. Soon the four of us were laughing and toasting Greece.

Isabelle ordered more wine.

As she poured, she asked our fellow diners what they thought of the idea of a three-way marriage, one man and two women. Did they think it could work? The husband chuckled and said it sounded *magnifique*, but he didn't believe such an arrangement could endure. His wife agreed. Jealousy would destroy it in the end. *"Ah, mais cet homme-ci,"* Isabelle said, pointing at me, "This man here thinks it can work. Don't you, David?"

"Don't start, Isabelle. I think no such thing."

"He has a wife in Africa and here he is in Greece with me. Isn't that, oh, I don't know — just so contemporary?"

I said, "More wine, anyone?"

"David left his wife for me. But he didn't really leave her, you see. He's here with me now, though not completely, and we're going to live on Callisto. But really, you see, David's on his way to Africa. So he'll spend some time with me, and then he'll go and live with his wife in Wajadili. He's got it all worked out."

Isabelle rambled on, impossible to stop, about how maybe she'd join me and my wife in Africa, but then again, maybe she wouldn't. Finally, having exchanged some private signal, the couple stood up as one. The wife said they'd enjoyed meeting us but had a busy day tomorrow. The husband, smiling tightly, tossed some American money onto the table. Then they were gone.

Seething, I paid the bill and strode back to the cabin without speaking. Once inside, Isabelle started in again, repeating her performance in soliloquoy. Maybe she'd join me and my wife in Africa, maybe she wouldn't. My head hurts to think about it. I reminded her, nastily, that she was the one who'd insisted on making this trip. That I'd been willing to call it quits in Montreal but she'd refused to let me go.

Isabelle lost control. She came at me red-faced and flailing, yelling: "You blockhead! You god-damn blockhead!" She knocked me into the wall and kept coming, slapping at my face. I ducked and she smacked the wall and fell onto the bunk, holding her hand and screaming like a fishwife. I backed out of the cabin while she yelled that she should have listened to her friends, I was just a god-damn English blockhead.

Up on deck, breathing through clenched teeth, I thought: *enough*. Tomorrow, when the ferry reached Callisto, I'd say goodbye to Isabelle. Stay on board and return to Athens. Isabelle could remain alone on the island. I'd fly straight to Wajadili.

For half an hour, muttering to myself, I tramped around on deck. Finally a group of Australians hailed me. They were passing around a gallon jug of red wine and invited me to join them. Two hours later, when I stumbled into the cabin, Isabelle was in bed. I climbed into my bunk, closed my eyes and felt the ferry rocking into the night.

In the darkness, the cabin began to spin. I stumbled into the bathroom and hung over the toilet bowl, miserable. Twice more that night I was sick. Come morning, badly hung over, I couldn't walk without clutching my sides. Isabelle and I weren't speaking. As the ferry boat churned into the port city of Palamedes — Callisto, ahoy! — she stood on one side of the deck and I stood on the other.

12 / BIRTH OF A BOOKSTORE

Quarter to six, David thought as he placed a too-hot cup of coffee on his desk. Suppertime. Hundreds of miles away, in northern Ontario, Arianna and the kids would just be sitting down. Suppertime at granny's. Instead of resuming his seat, David turned and crossed the living room to his tape collection. Often, when he felt low, he listened to golden-age Calypso music, precursor of rap, and now he knelt and hunted through tapes for an ancient favorite, a long-ago gift from Emmanuel Tolbert.

David had organized his collection by styles of music — Jazz, Rock, Classical, Blues — but one of the kids, probably Emile, had obviously been poking around. The realization brought not irritation but the threat of tears, and David willed himself to think about something, anything else. He remembered *The Montreal Standard* and, in his mind's eye, again saw the managing editor emerge from his office, walk to the centre of the newsroom and beckon all staffers into a semi-circle.

September, 1979. When the eight-month strike had ended, readers had come flocking back to *The Standard*. But English Montreal could no longer support two broadsheets, and the rival *Chronicle* had offered advertisers rock-bottom rates for long-term agreements. Lately, the rumor mill had been churning.

Still, even the gloomiest of his colleagues expected nothing worse than that the *Chronicle* might come aboard as a junior partner. *The Standard*, after all, had always been number one.

When the managing editor emerged, then, and beckoned everybody into the centre of the newsroom, David expected a big announcement. But nothing like: "*The Montreal Standard* is dead." Nothing like: "The company will treat you all fairly, give you all generous severance packages." Nothing like: "You've got half an hour. Clean out your desks and go home."

Ten minutes before, he'd been wrestling with a nostalgia piece on the music scene in Montreal, trying to decide whether to lead with the Esquire Showbar or Rockhead's Paradise. Funny, the things you remembered. When the managing editor emerged from his office, the movie critic had been talking to a contact in Hollywood. David had yelled at him but he didn't hang up until too late: "Dead? What do you mean, dead?"

As he crossed the newsroom, returning to his desk, David heard a silent ringing — as if he had water in his ears, or were seated in an airplane that was starting its descent. He stared, baffled, at his desk, the notes and files suddenly meaningless. The Esquire Showbar? Rockhead's Paradise? As he picked up the phone to call home, he noticed he was moving in slow motion.

When Arianna answered, the silent ringing stopped and he snapped back into real time. He could hear Emile, three months old, howling in the kitchen. "Arianna, you'd better sit down."

As David relayed the shocking news, strangers arrived — muscular men in blue uniforms. Stationed themselves around the newsroom. That was how the world ended, he thought now. Not with a bang but a rent-a-cop.

Like most *Standard* staffers, David applied to *The Chronicle*. But an old enemy from *The Toronto Tribune,* a man he'd once publicly denounced as an incompetent, had somehow become managing editor. Keeper of the gate. David tried to go over his head and failed. What to do?

From outside the province, two dailies came staff-hunting: *The Toronto Tribune* and *The Calgary Times.* Arianna detested Toronto, so grey and anonymous and ugly. But Calgary she'd consider. As a child, before moving to Ontario and then Quebec, she'd lived there for a year. Endless sunshine, she remembered. Big, big sky and the Canadian Rockies on the horizon.

David vetoed any move at all. They'd remained in Montreal through an eight-month strike and his feelings hadn't changed. Leave Montreal? No chance. Several months before, with Emile on the way, they'd scraped together a downpayment — Arianna's doing, mostly — and bought this semi-detached house on Old Orchard Avenue. And David's parents, built-in babysitters, still lived in Verdun, a bus ticket away. Arianna, now on maternity leave, would resume working in January. They'd remain in Montreal. If he couldn't find a job, he'd create one.

Now, in 1989, remembering, David discovered a small irony: Isabelle's destructive novel had made the bookstore possible. Because if, when *The Standard* died, he'd still been writing fiction, he'd have found another way to help pay the mortgage — maybe worked as a mailman — and for the rest done exactly what he did through the strike: sat at a desk and blackened pages. As it was, shut down as a fiction writer, David could imagine trying something new.

The Montreal Standard paid its employees lump-sum settlements based on salary and years of service. David received seven thousand dollars, and Emmanuel Tolbert, who was snapped up by *The Chronicle*, more than twelve. To Tolbert, David said: "Remember that bookstore we talked about?"

What Montreal needed, the two agreed once more, was a bookstore specializing in Canadian, Caribbean and First Nations Books. Bring on the awareness. But where to locate? Obviously, they needed an English area. Trouble was, Westmount had Black Water Books and downtown, Pages on Mansfield — both outstanding independents.

David figured Notre-Dame-de-Grace was ripe. Why not find a spot around Sherbrooke and Claremont, a welter of banks and pharmacies, restaurants, grocery stores and art galleries. Plenty of walk-in traffic and, not incidentally, an easy hike from Old Orchard Avenue. He was still hunting for the right space, though, when Tolbert found the perfect spot in the McGill Ghetto — a small redbrick building that had once housed a sandwich shop.

Further east on Milton, a second-hand bookstore was thriving. But that was just another reason to go ahead: non-competing bookstores loved company. True, Pages on Mansfield was just a few blocks south, but surely there was room in the Ghetto for a specialized store? David and Tolbert kicked in seven thousand each.

And in the summer of 1980, shortly after Quebec voted NON in its first referendum — NON, Quebecers did not want to separate from Canada — the bookstore was born: Calypso Canada Books. Why not?

13 / ISABELLE'S VOODOO

Flash back to early 1975 and for the past several months David and Arianna, happily married, have been talking New York City. David has set his novel-in-progress mostly in Greenwich Village, where at age nineteen he sojourned for three months. Arianna has visited the Big Apple only once and can talk of nothing but art galleries. As winter becomes spring and the school year winds down, they decide to drive down for a visit, why not? And blow their savings on a third-hand Volkswagen fastback.

Remembering now, in the empty house on Old Orchard, David picked up his rediscovered bongo drums and began slapping away, settling into an easy Calypso rhythm. Happily married, yes — until he'd decided he could have it both ways. He'd begun visiting Isabelle every second or third afternoon, taking her to bed and then listening to her talk. By the spring of 1975, he knew all about her marriage. Knew how, on the rebound in Paris, she'd found Kurt and gotten pregnant.

David knew that Kurt's mother maintained, no matter what her son said, that Isabelle had tricked him into marriage. He knew, too, how horribly Kurt had behaved when their sons were born (he was phobic about hospitals and didn't attend the births) and also how shamefully he'd treated Isabelle when he finally departed (the only way he could find, David understood now, to make her let go).

David knew all about the intense love affair that preceded the marriage, including how it ended: with Isabelle following the poor devil around Paris, refusing to accept his departure, instigating shouting matches in Metro stations and turning up at parties to which she hadn't been invited. At the last of these, she'd commandeered a bedroom, hiked up her skirt and spread her legs for every man who walked through the door.

Isabelle rambled obsessively about her "demons" and "other selves," and finally David understood that she wasn't speaking figuratively. She lived in a world of omens and mirror images, premonitions and synchronicities. In David, she'd found a would-be witch doctor, someone young enough to dream he could solve her mental problems where professionals had failed. His salad-days experiments with psychedelic drugs enabled him to understand her talk of perceptual shifts, of walls looming threateningly and faces changing shape, and surely understanding was just one step from healing?

David visited the occasional evening, as well, though Isabelle complained bitterly when he said he had to leave, rolled out of bed and pulled on his jeans. Then her friend Lachapelle got an out-of-town assignment and she suggested that they spend a night at his apartment: "Imagine, David. No interruptions. No leaving early. A whole night together."

David told Arianna that Tolbert needed help renovating an old farmhouse he'd bought near St-Eustache. Big, heavy job, he explained. Arianna said fine, no problem. And that weekend, he did visit Tolbert. Pounded a few nails.

But first he spent a night with Isabelle.

Three days before leaving for New York, David met Isabelle for coffee on Rue Laurier. Their favorite bistro: walking distance to her Outremont house, and far enough away from Concordia that they wouldn't run into anybody they knew. David told Isabelle he felt torn, that in New York he'd miss her terribly.

"David, I have something to tell you." Isabelle looked at the floor. "It's about T.J."

Poor old T.J. never does turn up in *Le Diable Entre Nous,* David reflected in west-end Montreal. Doesn't even get a walk-on under a phoney name. Come to think of it, this was understandable. You can't have a feminist saint balling her brains out with two husbands at once, neither one of them hers, either for its own sake or because she's using one man to make the other jealous. No, no, it just wouldn't wash.

But David could afford to remember T.J. — the only other married man in Paul Emmett's novel-writing workshop. He was in his early thirties, short and tough-looking with a square beard and a tattoo on his left forearm. Once a golden-gloves boxer, now T.J. drove a cab at night. Called it "a hack."

He'd set his novel-in-progress in northern Ontario, where he'd grown up as a foster child. David had recognized the geography —

Arianna's mother lived in Timmins — and invited T.J. for a beer. So began the tradition of visiting the Rymark for post-workshop drinks.

To Isabelle, in the bistro on Laurier, David said: "T.J.? What about T.J.?"

"Sometimes, at night, he stops by the house."

"What do you mean? To talk?"

Isabelle didn't look up. "I don't love him, David. I was trying to distance myself from you."

"You're telling me you've been sleeping with T.J.? I don't believe it."

"Put yourself in my place, David. You've got a wife."

"How long has this been going on?"

"What am I supposed to do? Sit at home while you're gadding about with Arianna?"

"Do you enjoy it, Isabelle?" Usually, he and Isabelle spoke in the language of their immediate environment, but now David switched to English and brought Isabelle with him. "Do you enjoy sleeping with T.J.?"

"It's not the same, David."

"This cock, that cock — what's the difference, eh?"

"With T.J., I don't... I don't do everything I do with you."

"What do you mean, Isabelle?" David heard his voice rising, fought for control. "You mean you don't perform oral sex?"

"David, I don't ask what you do with Arianna."

"So you do! You do it all!"

"If you must know, I don't let him take me from behind."

"You don't?" He tried for sarcasm but achieved only petulance. "Now I'm curious, Isabelle. Why don't you let him take you from behind?"

"To tell the truth, I don't trust him. The other day he got furious. 'I bet you let Nelligan do it,' he said. 'I bet you let Nelligan take you any way he wants.' It was scary."

"T.J. knows about me?" The words came out strangled.

"He told me not to tell you."

"Let me get this straight. You've not only been sleeping with T.J., but talking with him about me?"

"He guessed the truth, David. I told him I was in love. Anyway, I'm a single woman, remember? You've got a wife."

In retrospect, David had to admire her timing. In three days, with Arianna, he'd be visiting The Big Apple for the first time in years — and suddenly he could think of nothing but Isabelle in bed with T.J.

That night, David didn't sleep. The next he had a nightmare — stalled the Volkswagen in a tunnel, traffic bearing down — and woke up yelling. The morning he left with Arianna, David insisted on swinging past Isabelle's house to drop off a book. Arianna got talking architecture with the professor who shared the house, and David cornered Isabelle in the kitchen.

"I want you to stop seeing T.J."

"This is not the time, David. Go to New York and have a wonderful time. Write me a letter, *d'accord?*"

"I had a nightmare. I stalled the Volks in a tunnel. Trucks and buses bearing down."

"Will you bring me a present, David? Something small?"

So the trip began. David fumed while Arianna drove south to the American border. Rattled by his mood, she tried to navigate the crossing in third gear and stalled out. David yelled, "Put it in first, for god's sake."

She told him not to speak to her like that. For half an hour they drove in silence. Then David, who'd taken the wheel just beyond the border, put his foot to the floor and earned himself a sixty-dollar speeding ticket, payable on the spot. The silence grew louder.

Approaching New York City, driven by necessity — "Which way's Broadway? Is that Fifth Avenue?" — they resumed speaking. They'd reserved a room on the outskirts of Greenwich Village and, after checking in, began to feel better. Spent the evening poking around the district.

Still, David couldn't shake Isabelle. All night, again, he tossed and turned: kept seeing her in bed with T.J. Next morning, Arianna went gallery-hopping and David rambled around the Village, scribbling notes. He found an old haunt, a cheap restaurant off MacDougall, and wrote Isabelle the letter she'd requested.

Now, in west-end Montreal, pleased with himself for being a packrat, David studied a rough draft. "This out of the Village," he'd written, "over scrambled eggs, toast and coffee. I'm battling a jukebox. The weather is nothing but clouds. New York City is the same and yet different. The skyscrapers, the throngs — my preoccupations."

He couldn't decipher the next stretch. Too heavily edited. Something about getting a stalled Volkswagen out of a tunnel and a ritualized confession: "I see you naked on your bed, lotus-positioned. Me fully-clothed, my back against the headboard, drinking from a cup of dry red wine. Sound like fun?" He'd ended with a melodramatic flourish: "T.J. and I are enemies forever."

Now, David could only shake his head. Yet, after mailing this missive, he recalled, he felt better. He had one only more duty to perform. And, just before noon, in an-out-of-the-way curio shop, he found a voodoo doll from Haiti: carved and painted black, with string black hair and wearing beads — perfect. Having bought this and squirreled it away, the "small present" Isabelle wanted, David at last felt free to enjoy himself.

That afternoon, he and Arianna visited the Empire State Building — why not? Then they wandered into a bistro and had a few drinks, ended up splurging on a fancy dinner in a little Italian place. They'd been working too hard, they agreed. They owed themselves a good time. And for the next three days they played tourist: Times Square, Central Park, Radio City Music Hall, the Museum of Modern Art, up Fifth Avenue and down Broadway. They circle-cruised around Manhattan, rode the ferry to Staten Island, climbed inside the Statue of Liberty.

Two days before they'd planned to return home, they packed a picnic lunch and rode the subway to Coney Island. Ankle deep in the water, staring out, David had a moment of lucidity. Realized he was off-balance. But also that, if he stayed away from Isabelle a while longer, he'd regain his equilibrium. Back on the beach, he suggested to Arianna that they extend their holiday. Instead of driving home to Montreal, they'd visit Boston — or maybe Cape Cod.

Arianna said, "What about the garden party?"

An event Tolbert had been planning for weeks.

"We'll skip it," David said. "He's invited a hundred people. Won't even notice."

"Of course he'll notice. You helped him fix up the place, remember? Anyway, we said we'd be there. We can't just skip it."

14 / RENT MONEY

No doubt about it: Arianna was more considerate than he would ever be. As soon as he thought this, David wished he hadn't, because suddenly the house felt empty again. Empty and too quiet. He rose from his desk to ramble from room to room. Wintertime in Montreal. Nothing but cold, blowing snow and the whirr of the aging furnace.

Still, even winter had its moments. David reminded himself again of the previous week, that glorious sunny day when he'd visited Ste-Thérèse. He'd ended up driving down *Avenue des Anges* to the lake and parking in front of the summer camp where Old Pelletier once lived.

To get onto the beach he had to climb over a grass-covered dyke that hadn't existed when he was a boy. He understood the need for this barrier — how else to stop the annual flooding? — but hated it just the same. More than anything else, the dyke had transformed Ste-Thérèse into just another tacky suburb. Time was, you could see the lake from the highway simply by looking down any street. Now, you saw nothing but dyke.

The beach was smaller than David remembered, much of it overgrown by trees and bushes. Where once the sand had been clean and dry and so abundant you could bury friends or build giant castles, now it was hard-packed and patchy with weeds, bottle-strewn. A weathered sign declared: *"Defense de nager."* Gratuitous, really. Everybody knew the lake was polluted.

At least the view was unchanged: nothing discernible on the far shore, two or three miles distant, except a water tower and a few highrises. David remembered playing tag here on the beach in summer, and hockey in winter, on a makeshift rink. And as he stood looking out over the grey-green water, choppy in the breeze, he thought again — though he didn't know why — of the rent money he'd lost long ago.

"Mr. Noble, I've been robbed!"

"Are you trying to break down the door?" The principal stared down at him through thick glasses, his eyes huge and blue and watery. "Come in, then."

The principal closed the door and motioned him into a chair, then sat down behind his desk. "Now, David, what's happened."

"I've been robbed. I — "

"You mean something is missing. Don't be too anxious to accuse." He leaned forward and made a steeple with his fingers. "Now, what's missing?"

"Forty dollars."

Mr. Noble's eyebrows went up.

"I had it in my wallet. Now it's gone. I want to talk to my mother."

"What were you doing, carrying that much money?"

"It was rent money. I was supposed to deliver it."

"Where did you lose this rent money?"

"In the locker room." His voice quavered. "I went to basketball practice and ... and I left it in my locker."

"Ahhhhh." Mr. Noble leaned back in his chair and crossed his arms. "Now we're getting to it. You forgot to lock your locker."

David looked at the floor and nodded.

"How many times do I have to tell you people? Never leave your lockers unlocked. Never, never, never."

"Mr. Noble, could I use your telephone, please?"

"All right, David, go ahead." Mr. Noble left his desk, went to the window and stood looking out, his hands clasped behind his back.

The newspaper route. That was the connection, David realized at the beach. That was why the rent money came back. Often, after delivering at Old Pelletier's, David would stand and stare out over the lake, just as he was doing now. In winter, he could see nothing, of course. Yet he'd stand here anyway, stand and stare into the early-morning darkness.

Now it was winter that returned — all of winter resumed in a single morning: the cold, the dark, the blowing snow. David walked with his eyes closed, the wind at his back, listening to the crunch, crunch, crunch of snow beneath his feet. He heard a car coming. He opened one eye, saw Leroux's taxi, its diamond roof-light glowing orange through the snow, fish-tailing up the street towards him, taking Mr. Boyd to the train in Bonaventure. David moved over and let the taxi pass, then stepped into one of the tracks it had made and again closed his eyes.

In a couple of months, as soon as the roads were free of snow, he'd get out his bicycle. He'd be looking forward to an explosion of new orders from summer people, and also to delivering in daylight.

The only problem with spring was the lake. Often it overflowed the town as snow and ice melted. Sometimes the water came no farther than the crossroads, about a third of the way to the highway, and he could reach even his hardest-hit customers by wearing hip-waders. Usually, though, the lake washed past the Nelligan house at a depth of six or eight inches — turned the place into an island.

His mother would borrow a flatboat from Mrs. Middleton on the understanding that if the flood reached her house, she got it back. To deliver the newspapers, David would climb into the flatboat with his bicycle and pole his way up the street to water's edge, where the truck driver would have deposited the papers. He'd leave the flatboat there, deliver the top half of his route by bike, then return and do the rest by boat.

One morning he arrived at water's edge and found the flatboat gone. Had to stand there hollering until his mother heard him. Luckily, the Nelligans had a second borrowed boat tied up out front that week, a big old rowboat that had to be bailed out every two or three hundred yards. His mother rowed out and picked him up. He dropped her at the house, along with his bicycle, and then, to finish delivering, rowed on down *Avenue des Oracles*.

People rose early during the flood, and David asked everybody he met about the flatboat. Finally, Mrs. Boyd said she'd seen three men, summer people, pole by in it. She'd assumed they had permission. They hadn't? Talk about nerve!

David finished delivering at Old Pelletier's and rowed along the lakefront, bailing when necessary. Near the bottom of *Avenue des Anges*, he spotted the missing flatboat, tied up outside a flooded summer camp. Inside the house, three men were splashing around, cursing and and swearing, moving furniture. David sat a moment, thinking. The summer camp was up on stilts. Inside, he'd guess, the water was six inches deep. That made it chest deep out here. Departure would be cold and uncomfortable — but not impossible.

Quietly, David climbed into the flatboat and untied it. Then, towing the leaky rowboat, chortling, he poled up the street for home.

So much for spring. This was winter, and at *Monsieur Therrien*'s, if the dog was out, David would leave the *Chronicle* in the box at the fence. No sign of the beast, though, so he marched through the gate and up the path, climbed the back stairs. *Monsieur Therrien* was bent over the oil stove, his back to the door. David knocked. *Monsieur Therrien* yelled at the dog to shut up, then opened the door a crack. David handed him the *Chronicle*. "Want your driveway shovelled this afternoon?"

"Not today, David. I'm taking the day off."

David waved, went down the stairs and back out the gate, shutting it carefully so *Monsieur Therrien*'s dog wouldn't get out later. That was the trouble with odd jobs, he thought as he swung onto the street. He needed something he could count on.

"Mum? It's me, David."

"David? Is something wrong?"

"Mum, I've lost the rent money."

"The rent money?"

"I've lost it."

"What? All of it?"

"Yes, mum." His voice broke. "I forgot to lock my locker. When I checked after practice, the money was gone."

"Okay, David. Don't cry."

"Mum, what are we going to do?"

"Don't worry, David. I'll think of something. We're always a little behind."

"I'll pay it back, Mum."

"Don't talk foolishness. And stop crying, now. Where are you calling from."

"The principal's office. Mum, I'll pay it back."

"Stop crying, David, please. Go back to class now. Forget about the rent money."

"I'll pay it back, Mum. I'll pay it back."

Carefully, David deposited Old Pelletier's paper on his back porch, under the rug. Then he went down the steps and paused automatically, stared out over the frozen lake into the swirling blackness. Already he'd saved nine dollars, almost a quarter of what he'd lost. David pulled his scarf over his face and, leaning into the storm, started back up *Avenue des Oracles.*

No way he could quit delivering now. Maybe after he paid back the rent money. Except then it would be spring. He'd have a rash of new orders coming. He'd be able to ride his bicycle, and the sun would come up while he delivered.

15 / THE WOODEN SIGN

"You're an Anglophone, David. A blockhead."

"Arianna, I'm half-Québécois. Speak fluent French."

"And live mostly in English. Don't you get it? You're not wanted here."

"Not by a vocal minority, perhaps. But no way they're driving me out."

"What about the kids, David?"

"What about them? In Montreal they can grow up bilingual."

"Yes — and become second-class citizens."

This was late the previous night, David's second long-distance chat with Arianna — the one that haunted him. That began well and deteriorated.

"Remember the year we lived in Banff, David? How protected we felt?"

"The cabin on Wolf Street? Of course I remember. But listen, once — "

"The bookstore's history, David. If we sold the house — "

"Once the arson's sorted out, the insurance company will reimburse us. We'll rebuild here in Montreal."

"David, listen. If we sold the house we could relocate. Ship the furniture and drive out. I could get a designing job tomorrow. Or else start my own company. You could open a bookstore."

"Arianna, we've gone over this. In Montreal, by running an English-language bookstore, we're making a political statement. In Calgary or Banff, a bookstore would be just another business."

"Not quite. But forget the bookstore. Go back to journalism."

"I have roots here, Arianna. I can walk the streets and see where my father played Kick The Can in the alleys, and my grandfather before him."

"You're an Anglophone, David. A blockhead."

Round they went. In the end, they'd hung up angry. David told himself Arianna needed time, that was all. And realized he was rubbing his arms — that he felt cold. Already he'd donned a second sweater. Wintertime in Montreal.

From a hall cupboard, he removed a six-inch pile of yellowing newspapers. Arianna would get over this. She'd got over the trouble with the wooden sign, hadn't she? He carried the papers into the living room and began pulling them apart, tying pages into knots and tossing them into the fireplace.

Arianna had created the sign as a surprise birthday present. She'd lugged a sheet of three-quarter-inch plywood into her workshop and attacked it with a jigsaw. Then painted it. Big red letters on a white background: *"Librairie Calypso Canada / Calypso Canada Books."*

They'd been in business three weeks, making do with a rough cardboard sign, French-only. David had made it himself. Having invested their life savings, he'd grown suddenly cautious. Feared that a bilingual sign would provoke needlessly.

The permanent sign, he knew, would have to include English. Even so, at the sight of Arianna's big wooden sign, unveiled to him and Tolbert as a surprise, David sucked in his breath. She'd painted it in red and white, which suggested Canada. Worse, she'd made the English letters just as big as the French ones. This was clearly intentional, and would be read, no question, as arrogant and aggressive.

Arianna said: "Don't you like it?"

"Looks great. It's just, well, a bit risky."

Exasperated, Tolbert weighed in: "What kind of wimp are you turning into, David? Bookstores are exempt, remember? We're a cultural enterprise."

"I know that, Tolbert. But not everybody else does."

"Let's hang it," Arianna said, "and see what happens."

In the end, they mounted the sign out front.

Three days later, vandals ripped it down.

David discovered this, and also a broken plate-glass window, when he arrived one morning to open the bookstore. He called the police and then Arianna and Tolbert, who turned up separately minutes before the blue-and-white squad car.

"Monsieur Nelligan?" The officer who spoke was the older of the two. *"C'est vous qui a telephoné?"*

The police had parked their car directly in front of the bookstore. David was sweeping glass off the sidewalk. The cop glanced at the broken window, then at the glass, and flipped open his notebook. *"Qu'est-ce-qui est arrivé?"*

"See for yourself," David responded in French. "When I arrived to open the store I discovered this." He jerked his thumb at the broken window. Looked like they'd used a baseball bat. "And also that." He pointed at the redbrick wall above the window, where now an ugly strip of tar ran half the width of the store.

The policeman said: "That's the sign, there?"

David nodded. "One of our customers spotted it in a parking lot a couple of streets over. She phoned and my partner here" — he indicated Tolbert, who'd moved into the doorway— "went and got it."

Tolbert had leaned the sign against the front wall, its back to the street. The cop reached over, pulled the sign away from the wall and read aloud: *"Librarie Calypso Canada / Calypso Canada Books."*

He let the sign fall back against the wall, sighed and flipped his notebook shut. "The sign's illegal," he said. "What did you expect?"

"That sign's perfectly legal," Arianna declared flatly. "This is a bookstore."

In English, despite having promised to keep his mouth shut, Tolbert said: "We expect the police to protect the citizens of this province. That's what we expect."

"C'est qui, ça?"

"Mon partenaire." David gave Tolbert a look but his friend ignored it, said: "Never mind the sign. That plate glass window cost three hundred bucks."

In English, brightly, David said, "Tolbert, do you think you're helping?"

"I'll report the vandalism, monsieur, because I know that otherwise you'll have trouble collecting on your insurance." The cop stuffed his notebook into his pocket. "But I'd advise you to accept *La Loi 101.*"

16 / TROUBLE IN APOLAKIA

While crossing the Atlantic, Isabelle and I had planned our arrival on the island of Callisto. Now, having reached the port city of Palamedes, and despite a lingering coolness between us, we followed the script. If only because it was easier. So, while Isabelle waited on the ferry dock with our gear, I hitched into town. Got a ride in the back of a pick-up truck. Rough and bumpy, but the wind in my face made me feel better. Also, just being on land. I found the Avis office, rented a car and returned to collect Isabelle.

With the help of a passing teenager, I hoisted her trunk onto the roof rack and secured it. Off we drove, then, speaking only when necessary. Gradually, our mood lifted. Here we were on Callisto, after all, driving south towards the coast. We stopped for coffee at a roadside café. Responding to the friendly curiosity of the proprietor, we became civil. By the time we arrived in Apolakia, we were almost friends again.

We explored the touristy heart of town and hated it. Then, rambling back streets, we found the flat I've already described. And took it. Three days later, at my insistence — hadn't we come here to write books? — we launched into our routine.

This meant rising daily at six and, coffee in hand, withdrawing to our respective studies. At nine o'clock I would leave my typewriter and head down the street to the bakery. I loved this outing: women and children working and playing in the street, and donkeys braying, a strange heaving sound I'd never heard before.

Too quickly, I'd reach and enter the small, dark bakery, my mouth watering at the smell of fresh-baked bread. I'd buy feathery rolls hot out of the oven and, back in the flat, we'd eat them for breakfast, still warm, with marmalade and coffee.

Then it was back to work until noon, when I'd make lunch at the hotplate — soup and sandwiches, or else spaghetti out of a tin. After lunch, back to work. I'd knock off around two-thirty — before Isabelle — and change into my swimming trunks. I'd check that my snorkle, mask and fins were in my little green knapsack, along with pencil and paper, then swing down the narrow, white-washed street to climb the hill that overlooked the harbour.

There, beside the stone sentry box built during the Second World War, I'd sit gazing out over the Mediterranean. For a while I'd scribble notes about my work-in-progress, and then I'd give myself over to my deeper preoccupation — Arianna.

Banff would come to me often. I'd remember our little cabin on a back street in town, looking out the window at the moon. And the night we skated, just the two of us, alone on a deserted pond under the stars. Visiting our favorite spot along the Bow River. And walking, early morning, to the Banff Springs Hotel and our jobs in the kitchen, always a light snow falling.

And before that, Montreal. Skiing with Arianna Larivière in the Laurentians, though really this meant Arianna giving me lessons. Leaving early from the house she shared with another university student and stopping for pancakes on the highway to Mont Tremblant. An expert slope we ventured onto "by accident," and Arianna laughing until she cried, urging me to take off my skis and walk down. How I refused to listen. So many good times. Hard times, too — but times together. I vowed to make them come again.

At three-thirty I'd scramble down the hill. I'd meet Isabelle at the circular bench in the square and together we'd go to the beach. For half an hour I'd swim alone, the water cold and choppy, and then I'd join Isabelle on shore. When we got too hot, we'd head for the town square, choose one of the outdoor cafés and sit drinking ouzo.

When we saw the bus arrive from Palamedes, we'd knock back the last of our drinks. On our way home we'd buy what we needed for supper — I'd learned enough Greek to negotiate prices — and stop at the post office to collect our mail.

While Isabelle cooked supper — I made breakfast and lunch, after all — I'd retreat into my study with Arianna's letters. This made Isabelle furious, I knew, but when was I going to read them? I refused on principal to cut into my writing time — though, also, it's true, I couldn't wait. Arianna in Africa! How was she faring?

After supper, I'd wash and dry the day's dishes. Then we'd read and talk books until ten o'clock, bed-time. Saturday nights we'd splurge and dine at a taverna. And Sundays we'd take the afternoon off and head farther along the beach to where we could swim nude.

It was an insane schedule and not much like a holiday. But Isabelle had convinced me that moving to Africa with an unfinished manuscript would be like jumping off a balcony in the eighth month of a pregnancy, and I meant to finish my rewrite before Christmas.

Now I can admit that this was only part of my workaholism. I was also trying, with this schedule, to preclude greater intimacy — which is, of course, precisely what Isabelle sought. She still hoped I'd change my mind and decide to stay.

She was beginning to despair when she received a letter from the older sister of her friend Lachapelle. This woman had married a white Kenyan, lived in Nairobi and owned a cottage on the coast, near Mombasa — just two days drive from Wajadili. For months, Isabelle had been lobbying to borrow this cottage. I never thought she'd pull it off — though now I believe that if Arianna had landed a job in Tibet, Isabelle would have discovered a long-lost friend in nearby Bhutan.

Anyway, five weeks into Apolakia, she received this letter from Kenya saying no problem: Isabelle could borrow the cottage next spring. Right away, she began lamenting that, back in Montreal, she'd never really got to know Arianna. But look: the cottage in Kenya created new possibilities. Maybe we could all three get together there? See what happened?

If we can get together in Kenya, I said, why can't we do so in Greece? Maybe at Christmas? Arianna had mentioned wanting to see the islands. And Isabelle had been fretting about spending the holiday alone. If Arianna came up for Christmas, I'd remain in Apolakia through January — be able to finish my rewrite without feeling pressured. Isabelle and I elaborated this scenario while drinking ouzo at our favorite café.

Then I wrote Arianna. Meet me in Athens, I said, and we'll spend four or five days on the mainland, just the two of us. Playing tourist. Making love. I'd buy my airplane ticket to Wajadili, swing into the consulate and fill out the requisite forms. We'd catch the overnight ferry to Palamedes and ride a bouzouki-mad bus down the coast to Apolakia. Plenty of room in the flat for three. Arianna could have the big room to herself, and Isabelle and I would move into our respective studies.

We'd celebrate Christmas and New Year's in Apolakia. Then, at the end of January, I'd join her in Wajadili and we'd celebrate our anniversay. What was that Ernest Dowson line? "So seize the moment, while there is moment yet to seize."

Arianna wrote back saying no thanks. She'd love to visit Greece and longed to see me, but the idea of sharing a flat with Isabelle — well, it just wouldn't work. The sooner I came to Wajadili, the better.

At this I panicked — and came clean. Isabelle, too, had been having second thoughts. We'd always fought and argued, I wrote, but lately our battles had escalated. Isabelle was two people: the witty, charming and sophisticated woman of the world, and, well, this raging harpy. More and more often, lately, this Other Woman would take over and throw a tantrum like you wouldn't believe. It was scary. I didn't know what to do.

I hinted at emotional blackmail. I didn't say outright that Isabelle had threatened to kill herself if I left her alone. But I disclosed enough that Arianna became concerned — not for Dominique but for me. She didn't agree to come to Apolakia. But she bought a plane ticket to Athens. And I responded with relief:

All this yammering back and forth, getting ourselves worked up. I'm coming to Africa. Nothing can stop me. We'll be alone together. Is that what I want? Yes, I want to be alone with you, Arianna. To relax again, get back to myself.

I was thinking about this today, at the sentry box. All this agonizing. Point is, I'm coming to Africa no matter what. We'll be together in Wajadili. And first you'll visit Greece! Maybe we'll sail to Crete, rent a car and tool around? Isabelle was saying yesterday that she wouldn't want to join us in Athens. She understands that you and I need time alone. Ain't that the truth!

17 / DAVID TAKES A BEATING

Certain pivotal moments you recognize instantly. Others slip past, and you identify them only later. So David reflected as he stoked the fire on Old Orchard Avenue, remembering that moment in New York City when he and Arianna lay on the beach at Coney Island. If she'd agreed to extend their holiday — been less considerate, more selfish — they'd have skipped Tolbert's garden party. And had an extra week to rediscover each other. Maybe he would have evaded Isabelle altogether.

"So even now," came a voice from deep inside, "even now, after all these years, you're trying to absolve yourself. To blame Arianna, however subtly, for your shameful defection."

Aloud, David said: "I'm doing no such thing."

"I don't understand why you behaved as you did."

"That's because you don't want to believe in Isabelle's power. Or accept that she might crave victimization at the hands of men — if only for the sake of her art."

"And so drive them to it? No. I want more."

David threw up his hands: "I'm sorry but there IS no more."

He sat down in front of the blazing fire, wedged his bongo drums between his knees and revived the Calypso rhythm he'd discovered earlier. As it happened, the pivotal New York City moment slipped away.

Back in Montreal, at the bistro on *Rue Laurier,* Isabelle exclaimed happily over the voodoo doll he brought her. They had time only for a quick coffee, both of them committed elsewhere. While he was away, Isabelle said, she'd written him a long letter. Only now she didn't want him to read it. Laughing, David insisted. Finally, on condition that he read it later, after she left, she handed it over.

David opened the letter on *Rue Laurier* as soon as Isabelle drove off. Hungry for words of love, avid to hear how much she'd missed him, he began reading as he leaned against the Volkswagen in the sun. She'd written in French, of course. Sure enough, she'd imagined him striding around Manhattan, wild among the skyscrapers. She'd pictured him visiting art galleries, dining out in tiny, perfect restaurants. She wanted so much to go somewhere with him, to be with him when he didn't have to watch the clock, pull on his jeans and go home.

Isabelle longed to bring David to Ste-Adele, to her cabin, and lie with him out back in the long grass. Yes! She and Jacques Bienvenue, her ex-lover, and still a member of her circle of friends, had driven up north last weekend and done just that. What? David gripped the letter with both hands and read on, horrified. They'd brought a picnic lunch and a blanket and made love for old time's sake. That was how Jacques had put it, trying an English expression he'd seen in some movie, enjoying the idiomatic sound of it: "For old time's sake."

Made Isabelle laugh, the way he said it. They smoked grass and had a fine old time, she wrote. But it wasn't making love. No. Screwing was fun, but this other, this act she performed with David — that was incredible. The difference between black-and-white and technicolor movies.

Red-faced, disbelieving, David read on. The following day, back in Montreal, T.J. had visited and they'd talked for hours. T.J. needed her more than he did. David was very self-sufficient, did he realize that? Also, so open and demonstrative. T.J. couldn't show his feelings. He fought with his wife. Yet he loved her, Isabelle felt — however dissatisfied he might be, and however badly he behaved.

Isabelle implored him not to consider T.J. an enemy. Why should T.J. upset him? If David found Isabelle lovable, then surely he could understand that other men might feel the same? T.J. needed his friendship. If he'd told Isabelle to prevaricate, to say nothing of their relationship, remember this: she hadn't had to take his advice. Perhaps she'd wanted T.J. to manipulate her?

There was more, too much more.

That night, David went to bed with a headache. He lay awake all night, tossing and turning, imagining Isabelle making love with Jacques Bienvenue in the long grass at Ste-Adele. And what about this long talk with T.J.? By morning, David couldn't see straight. He'd forgotten New York City. Coney Island? What special moment?

Today was Tolbert's garden party. David would see Isabelle and tell her no more sleeping with Bienvenue or anybody else "for old time's sake." And no more long talks with T.J., either. He knew where long talks led.

That afternoon, when he and Arianna arrived at Tolbert's, having driven the long way to St-Eustache, thirty or forty people were already there. Half of them worked at *The Montreal Standard*, where Tolbert had begun making his name. A few came from the novel workshop — guys who'd met Tolbert through David. The others came from who knew where? Who cared?

Behind the farm house, among the pines and weeping willows, Tolbert had set out three kegs of beer and a washtub full of ice and soft drinks. He'd also rigged up a sound system, and over it blared a scratchy tape David hadn't heard before. Two women and a young guy in jean shorts were tossing a frisbee, playing pig in the middle.

David went into the kitchen, where several people were passing around joints. He chatted with two guys he'd known in high school. Arianna got talking with a sculptor, a woman she hadn't seen in years. Isabelle arrived with Philippe Lachapelle, her oldest friend — an unusually urbane nationalist, and safely gay. David excused himself and led her to a quiet corner in the living room, made her sit down.

"What happened with T.J.?"

"Pardon?"

"While I was in New York, Isabelle. Buying you presents. Did you sleep with him too?"

"None of your business."

"You did! You slept with him!"

"What are you saying, David? That I can't have male friends?"

"Male friends, no problem. Friends you don't sleep with."

"You have a wife, David, remember? You think — "

"Well, well, well. What do we have here?"

It was T.J. himself, pulling up a kitchen chair. He twirled it on one leg, then straddled it and leaned his elbows on the back: "Don't let me interrupt."

Isabelle said: "You told me you weren't coming. Where's your wife?"

"Changed my mind," he said. "She's at home."

David and T.J. glared at each other.

Isabelle said, "David, I'd love a glass of white wine. Would you mind?"

Near the refrigerator, where David had to wait in a small throng, two graduate students were debating the merits of Julio Cortazar and Gabriel Garcia Marquez. David declined to enter the fray. Through the kitchen window, he spotted Arianna out back, still talking with her sculptor friend. She waved and he waved back, pretended not to understand her motion to join them.

As he reached the wine table, David glanced into the living room. Saw Isabelle speak sharply to T.J. He shook his head no, adamant. She rose and strode across the room to Emmanuel Tolbert, who was laughing with a circle of newspaper types. She tugged at his shirt-sleeve, whispered in his ear, then led him down the hall — and into the bathroom?

After a couple of moments, T.J. marched down the hall and hammered on the bathroom door. "What's going on in there?"

No answer. T.J. discovered the bathroom light switch and flicked it up and down. Secretly, David approved. What *was* going on in there?

Eventually, Isabelle emerged. She'd been crying. She came to him: "David, I want to walk with you."

As they left, T.J. shouted after them: "O.K., Isabelle. If that's the way you want it."

Isabelle led David out the front door. They walked down the country road that ran into the town of St-Eustache, three miles away. Nothing to see but parked cars, fields and trees. Strangely silent, almost glazed, Isabelle clung to his arm. Said no, please, she didn't want to talk, just walk.

They passed another farmhouse, and then a rutted dirt road. Isabelle led him off this road into a stand of bushes. She leaned against him, began tugging at the zipper on his jeans. "Isabelle, knock it off. What are you doing?"

"Nothing. Maybe saying goodbye."

"Someone could come around that corner at any moment."

"I hope I'm not saying goodbye."

"You toked up, didn't you? Before you came to the party."

"Philippe and I shared a joint."

"Then you drank wine. Come on, Isabelle, knock it off."

Still strangely silent, preoccupied, Isabelle walked with David back towards the farmhouse. Two people stood on the porch, talking intensely. T.J. and Arianna. "So here's the famous feminist," Arianna said in English as they approached. "An inspiration to us all."

David said, "Arianna... "

"You shut up! T.J. told me everything. Our famous feminist here is nothing but a lying hypocrite. Pretends to be a friend when all the time she's sneaking around behind my back."

Isabelle said, "In a way, I am your friend."

"You're a bitch, Isabelle. A hypocritical, back-stabbing bitch."

"Okay, Arianna," David said. "This won't solve —"

"She'd never, ever take up with another woman's husband. Oh, no, not Isabelle Garneau." Arianna was shaking with anger, but imitated Isabelle beautifully, saying softly, wide-eyed: "I'm not into husbands."

David reached for her, "Arianna, let's —"

"Get your hands off me!"

"Take it easy, Arianna," T.J. said. "Together, we can straighten this out."

Half a dozen people had emerged from the house, attracted by the ruckus.

"This is none of your business," David said to T.J. "Why don't you get out of here?"

"This IS my business, pretty boy." T.J. took Isabelle by the arm. "Come on, Isabelle. I'll take you home. Let these lovebirds sort out their marriage."

"Get your hands off her," David said, and turned to Isabelle. "Why don't you tell him to get lost?"

"I'll tell you why, pretty boy. Because she loves me, too."

Isabelle stared at the ground.

"Go ahead," T.J. said. "Tell him what you told me."

"What's he talking about, Isabelle? Who *do* you love?"

"Come on, Isabelle," T.J. said. "We're waiting."

Finally, Isabelle looked up at T.J.: "It's useless, I know. But I love David."

T.J. spat on the ground. "Come on, Arianna. Let's get out of here."

David said: "I told you to get your hands off her."

T.J. punched him in the mouth. David tumbled backwards onto the lawn. He came off the grass at T.J. with everything he had. Somehow, he missed. He took one shot in the body and two more in the face before he went down again. Then T.J. was on him, smashing away.

Finally, Emmanuel Tolbert and two other guys dragged him off and held him. David's mouth was bleeding. He went to the bathroom to wash and, when he emerged, T.J. was gone. Tolbert was in the living room, talking with Arianna. Isabelle was in the kitchen, preparing to leave with Philippe Lachapelle. She came over and dabbed at his mouth with a handkerchief. "You must be crazy, David. You knew T.J. was a golden-gloves boxer."

"That bastard. Anyway, now it's out in the open."

"Will you visit me tomorrow?"

"Yes."

"Will you, David? Promise?"

"I promise."

As David spoke, Arianna appeared beside him. Her face was white. Ignoring Isabelle, she held out her hand: "Give me the car keys."

Isabelle left with Lachapelle.

Tolbert tried to convince Arianna to stay, insisted she wasn't fit to drive. Neither of them was fit to drive. Arianna wouldn't hear of remaining, though, and finally David left with her.

All the way into Montreal, they drove in silence.

Whenever he spoke, Arianna told him to shut his face.

That night, again, David slept on the couch.

Come morning, Arianna still refused to speak to him. Their apartment consisted of three rooms, but whenever he entered one of them, she left it. He sat in the living room drinking coffee, while Arianna opened and shut drawers in their bedroom. She was packing. He knocked on the bedroom door: "Arianna, we've got to talk."

"Go talk to Isabelle. You promised, remember?"

After a few moments, Arianna emerged carrying two suitcases. Her face was white. She marched past David to the door: "I'm taking the Volks."

"Arianna, wait." He grabbed her elbow. "Where are you going?"

Arianna put down her luggage. He thought she was stopping to talk, but she turned and slapped his face: "Now you've got something to tell that two-faced bitch."

She picked up her suitcases and walked out the door. David stood rubbing his face as her footsteps receded down the stairs. He went to the front window and stood behind the curtain, looking down onto Aylmer Street. He watched Arianna unlock the Volkswagen, load her suitcases into the back and climb into the front.

David heard the car start. He watched Arianna back into the street, then straighten out and drive off. Where was she going? For a long time, David stared into the street. What had he done?

18 / ADIEU, MONTREAL

"Come on, Dad. You miss Montreal something fierce. Why not admit it?"

"Not when I see what's happening, I don't. We're glad to be shut of it."

That was the surprise, David realized afterwards, when he sat at the kitchen table wolfing down a toasted bacon and tomato sandwich. His father's change of heart.

The phone call had whisked him back to the present, to 1989. His parents had brought him up to date while he sat imagining them in their cosy little house in St. Catharines, Ontario. His mother would be sitting in the living room, where in summer, the overhead fan whirling, the TV blaring, she avidly cheered the Toronto Blue Jays; his father upstairs in his study, surrounded by books and video tapes and old records.

Arthritis was bothering his mother, as it did every winter, but she'd bought some new medication and she'd see. Last week the furnace had died but a repairman had somehow revived it. They'd need a new one soon. But Arianna and the kids? When were they returning home?

"They'll stay in Timmins a while yet," David had said. "Until things settle down."

"I still think you should move to Ontario," his mother said. "People here are so friendly."

"We lived in Toronto, Mum, remember? Arianna hated it."

"Everyone speaks English. You aren't afraid to open your mouth in the grocery store."

"Toronto's too big," his father said. "Out here's much more liveable."

"Come on, Dad. You miss Montreal something fierce. Why not admit it?"

"Not when I see what's happening, I don't. We're glad to be shut of it."

David remembered their last walk around Montreal. That was what — 1981? Eight years before. A blustery October afternoon and his father reminiscing about growing up in the streets of the city, early nineteen-thirties: "Three times a week I went to the Fairyland Theatre, corner Inspector and Notre Dame. I went to the Lido, the Corona. They were further west along Notre Dame, between Guy and Atwater."

His father pointed. "For twelve cents, then fifteen, you could see a double feature with newsreels, a cartoon and a chapter of a serial. Tim McCoy, Hoot Gibson."

"Tom Mix." David had heard the story countless times, but found himself revelling in it anyway. "Where'd you get the money to go?"

"Maybe I'd find a beer bottle, bring it to the Handy Store. That was a nickel. One of the boarders might send me to the corner for cigarettes. Another five cents. My mother would make up the difference: *Tiens, Gerry. Ne sois pas trop tard.* Don't be late.' "

"Your mother didn't mind if you watched English movies?"

"You kidding? She encouraged it."

"Down the stairs you'd fly...."

"Down the stairs, out the door and around the corner onto Notre Dame. Who's telling this story? John Barrymore, Garry Cooper. To get into the theatre you had to be sixteen. I wore a fedora three sizes too big, pulled it down over my eyes. Dangled a cigarette butt from my lower lip."

The light turned green and they fought their way up the Peel-Street hill against the wind. "Cathedral Street was right over there." His father indicated the towering Hotel Bonaventure. "After school we'd gather in the back alley, every kid in the neighborhood. Play Hide and Seek, Red Rover, Kick The Can."

"Then the Depression hit," David said. "Nineteen thirty-five. Nobody could find a job."

His father paused as they crested the hill. "I started selling *Chronicles* right here, in front of Windsor Station. Bulldog edition. Pick them up there at Metropolitan News, ten o'clock at night. 'Paper mister?'"

He shook his head and resumed walking. "I tell you, David, there's history in these streets. I'm leaving part of myself behind."

David said nothing. What could he say?

For the past seventeen years, his father had worked for Canadian Guaranty Life Insurance. Handled public relations, edited the company newsletter. Now he was nearing sixty. No hope of landing another job, and not enough money in the bank to retire early.

Trouble was, Canadian Guaranty had decided to move St. Catharines. Quebec's new language laws prescribed French in the workplace, and the company did half its business south of the border. Switching to French would jeopardize that.

"Your mother will be glad to leave," his father said. "She was ready in the late sixties, when the FLQ started planting bombs in mailboxes. Or even earlier. After *La Victoire.*"

By now they were sitting in the Rymark Tavern, eating pickled eggs and drinking draft beer. His father's mood had darkened, but David ventured that, really, Anglophones had only themselves to blame: the new language laws were just chickens coming home to roost.

His father snorted: "Next you'll be telling me that English-speaking Quebecers are the best-treated minority in the world."

"We do have our own school system, Dad. Our own hospitals. Our own universities."

"Yes, and why not? Damn it, son, English-speakers built this city — the foundaries, the shipyards, the Lachine Canal, the Victoria Bridge. At the beginning of this century, Montreal was an English-speaking city."

"Dad, I know that." It was late afternoon and the Rymark was filling up. "Not so loud."

"Never mind, David. We still have freedom of speech, even in Quebec." His father took a swig of beer, then continued more quietly. "Turn on the radio and you've got the most popular FM station in Montreal pumping out American hits. They even lift interviews. The announcer does a voice-over paraphrase: '*Diana Ross a dit que, blah, blah, blah.*' The problem's not English Montrealers. The French are doing it to themselves."

"You're upset about leaving, Dad. I understand that."

But his father was on a roll: "Fact is, French-speaking Quebecers are themselves the best-treated minority in the world. They've not only been able to redefine themselves as a majority, but to create a provincial government bent on driving English-speakers out of a city they built."

"Nobody's driving the English out."

"No, of course not. The government is just making it so unpleasant for Anglophones to stay that we'll all just pack up and leave. Wake up, David! You've got a brother in Edmonton, two sisters in Vancouver. Now your mother and I are moving to Ontario."

"Nobody's driving you out."

"The hell they aren't!"

They looked at each other in surprise. Then David punched his father's shoulder: "We'll find ways of living together, Dad, French and English. If only because we have to."

"What about the bookstore?"

"What do you mean? It's doing great."

"The vandalism, I mean. The sign."

David waved his hand dismissively: "That could have happened anywhere."

His father sipped his beer, nodding. "I made the same choice myself, I guess." He stared off into space. "After *La Victoire.*"

19 / EXISTENTIAL HONEYMOON

Scratch an intimate relationship and you'll find an unwritten agreement. Keep scratching and you'll uncover the secret needs of its wouldn't-be signatories. Between David and Isabelle the deal was this: she'd understand that he was a young writer of extraordinary promise if he'd endorse the notion that she was sexually irresistible. She'd see him as a couldn't-miss novelist if he'd see her as a *femme fatale*.

It wasn't that they lied to each other. Isabelle did recognize his talent, whatever she wrote later, to hurt him. And, yes, the sex was good. David would respond to Isabelle's howling abandon, and she'd respond to his responding, and afterwards they'd wonder laughing what the boaters down by the wharf thought of the noise.

It wasn't that they lied to each other, then, but to themselves. Isabelle's self-deception stood revealed in *Le Diable Entre Nous*. Instead of acknowledging that she craved sexual reassurance, she cast herself as a blonde bombshell: sexy, sultry, supremely liberated. And the heroine's antagonist, except for being a superb lover, is such a negative figure that the small-mag reviewers scratched their heads: "What does she see in this jerk?"

As for David, his desire to be recognized as an author, as distinct from his need to write, drove him to deceive himself. Now, as he slapped away on his rediscovered bongos, crooning to himself, he began to understand. He'd bought into Isabelle's world and in the process sold out love.

First came the honeymoon, though, when he perceived Isabelle as a once-in-a-lifetime discovery, a globe-trotting intellectual who'd visited Africa, sojourned in Mexico, travelled alone around South America. Isabelle was a bohemian Jeanne Moreau, a sultry wearer of floor-length skirts from around the world. At the cottage in Ste-Adele, she read him poetry and brought him roses cut from a bush in the back yard.

Together they played word games, shifting between English and French, feeling superior to those who couldn't. If Isabelle was self-centred and inward-looking almost to illness, she was also articulate, entertaining, weirdly one of a kind. And initially David found it possible to share in her obsessions — first, with herself, or rather selves, and second, with the occult.

Mirror-writing, left-handedness, inverted symbols — these were everywhere in her novels. But he hadn't realized that, at her place in Ste-Adele, under a bunk in the writing shed, Isabelle kept a whole library of books on witchcraft. Or that she could ramble about it, as she did that first August, for hours on end.

Isabelle distinguished between sorcerers and witches. Sex had nothing to do with it. Sorcerers were ordinary people driven by envy, malice or a desire for revenge. To achieve their ends, they'd employ magic. Witches, on the other hand, were tragic, tortured figures, slaves of aberration and addiction. A witch might be unaware of her own nature, a vehicle for a greater power. She needed no medicine, no rite, no spell — nothing but her psyche. "The distinction is logically flawless," Isabelle insisted, "even if it's not true."

At other times, the two of them talked politics — specifically, Quebec independence. 1975, this was. The fledgling *Parti Québécois,* led by René Lévesque, was a weak-sister opposition party. Few believed it would form the next provincial government. "What if it did?" Isabelle asked. "Quebec's independence might be the best thing that ever happened to Canada."

David thought not. But why get worked up? He preferred to talk literature. A few years before, knocked out by James Joyce, he'd developed a notion of The Artist as someone above the fray, detached, paring his finger nails. Readers? They could come to him on his terms or not at all.

From this arrogance, newspapering had partially redeemed him. By the mid-seventies, he wanted to be accessible, at least. To reach an audience. But as yet he'd developed no new aesthetic.

Isabelle, meanwhile, whose fiction was both self-consciously feminist (hence, her use of witchcraft) and flagrantly autobiographical, had embraced *écriture au féminin*: *"Pas de Québec libre sans libération des femmes,"* she'd declare in moments of wine-fueled candor. *"Pas de femmes libre sans libération du Québec."*

At the Sorbonne, she'd written her thesis on feminist existential-ism. Often, to illustrate some point, she'd quote Simone de Beau-voir. Finally, in self-defence, David read de Beauvoir's *Second Sex*. He found the book windy, overblown, but it did rekindle his interest in existentialism. Years before, he'd chased the merry god-is-dead-ness of it backwards from Henry Miller to Dostoevsky, then forwards through Nietzsche to Heidegger and Sartre. This time around, with Isabelle at his elbow, he discovered the notion of *littérature engagée*.

Culture was not, as Joyce would have it, an externalized "some-thing out-there" from which the writer should stand apart, indiffer-ent. Culture was a living organism. The writer not only "belonged to" but was "part of" — and so had a responsibility.

With Isabelle that first summer, drunk on red wine, David raved that Canadian literature had gone astray when it turned its back on social reality and personal experience. Academic namby-pambies had taken over, word-game specialists who claimed literature was created only out of other literature. Partly that was true, he'd declare. But partly it was an excuse, a rationalization for academic writers who'd failed to engage with life, to live intensely, authenti-cally, and so had nothing to say.

Canadian literature needed novels that jumped out of the bushes and grabbed you by the throat — crazy, fearless novels that wrestled reality to the ground. Novels of the kind, you guessed it, he and Isabelle were writing. In bed, they'd end up toasting courage and honesty and commitment: "To *écriture au féminin!*"

"To *littérature engagée!* Authentic fiction!"

20 / TALKING CALYPSO

Tolbert tried to warn David about Isabelle, backing into it with a celebration of Calypso music. "Blues with a political dimension," he called it, crossing his ankles on a wooden crate that served as both footstool and coffee table in that dinky little apartment on Aylmer Street. Spring, 1975.

The summer before, Tolbert had visited Trinidad for the first time as an adult, boasting as he departed that he might never come back. On his return, he'd taken to wearing a lapel-pin on his favorite bomber jacket: a small Canadian flag. "Back home was nothing but parties and drinking rum and going to the beach on Sundays, mon," he'd say with a wink. "Me, I'm heavy into Protestant Work Ethic."

Now, with a cigarette in one hand, a bottle of beer in the other, Tolbert held forth while introducing a pirated cassette tape a cousin had sent him from Trinidad: golden-age Calypso from the nineteen thirties and forties. Dig the vitality, he told David — the tongue-in-cheek macho, the rhythmic richness.

Born in Trinidad, he said, Calypso harked back to drum-crazy Africa. Forget this tightass European approach, one rhythm per song: straight ahead, gentlemen, steady as she goes. Calypsos could feature two, three, even four different rhythms. When the Calypsonian who called himself Roaring Lion sang about Bing Crosby and the Four Mills Brothers, suddenly whap! change of pace! he'd break into a few bars of *Pennies From Heaven* or *Nobody Cares For Me*.

"Dig this," Tolbert said, as Attila the Hun and Roaring Lion began trading verses about an epic boxing match between Joe "The Bomber" Louis and Max Schmeling: *The critics said The Bomber lost the fight that night/ Because he couldn't stop Max's smashing right,/ Though a disappointment he has now faced/ He has been defeated but not disgraced.*

"Dialogues like this one," Tolbert said, "grew out of the drumming and chanting that accompanied traditional stick-fights. They outlawed the fighting, eventually, but the music evolved into duets and dramas and full-scale Calypso Wars — protracted battles in which singers argued and traded insults." He motioned David to silence and Attila sang: *He's now waging a come-back campaign,/*

And none can deny that he's making his name. Cut to Roaring Lion: *Whoever The Bomber meets, come what may,/ He means to overcome them, to kill and slay.*

Attila the Hun, Roaring Lion. Tolbert laughed and clapped his hands at the strutting, tongue-in-cheek macho of the pseudonyms. He loved the king-sized personae the Calypsonians created for themselves: The Destroyer, Lord Executor, Sir Lancelot. "Who you want to be?" he demanded. "Pick a name!"

"I don't know —Raging Goliath?"

"The Avenging Canuck?"

"The Mighty Hamlet?"

"Hey, I like that. Your constant vacillating. I dub thee Mighty Hamlet."

Tolbert turned, then, to the eclecticism of Calypso, extolling the way a singer could explore anything from water shortages to the state of the telephone system. One Calypsonian eulogized the Trinidad government's latest five-year plan, while another lamented the abdication of King Edward the Eighth of England.

"Nothing about Quebec separatism?"

"They've left that to Mighty Hamlet. But you do see my point? In Calypso, anything goes — from Shakespeare to separatism."

Again Tolbert gestured for silence and a passionate anti-colonialist called Lord Invader began complaining bitterly about a lost love: *She told me plainly, she loved Yankee money,/ And, she said, Lord Invader, money for to find rum and coca-cola,/ So don't bother, if you know you ain't got no Yankee dollar.*

Tolbert said: "That sense of engagement? That defiant topicality? That's unique to Calypso."

"What about Blues?"

"Blues doesn't wrestle with political issues. It hasn't got the range. Calypso is Blues with a political dimension."

"Okay, I'm sold."

"It's the voice of the man in the street crying, 'Look, mon! The emperor's mistress has no clothes!'"

After their fourth or fifth beer that Calypso afternoon, while rewinding the tape for the third time, Tolbert said that he'd recently quaffed beer at the Rymark with T.J.

"You drank with that scumbag?"

"He phoned and invited me and I went. He feels bad about what happened. David, you knew he was a golden-gloves boxer."

"He had no business opening his mouth to Arianna."

"You're bent on making him the villain of the piece."

"If it weren't for T.J., none of this would have happened."

"You sure you know what you're doing?"

"What do you mean?"

"Leaving Arianna for Isabelle."

"Arianna and I haven't been happening for years."

"That's not how it looked to me."

"I don't want to talk about it."

"Jesus, mon! How can you do this? I haven't read Isabelle's books but —"

"Tolbert, I don't want to talk about it."

"She's so driven, so obsessive — so fanatically self-absorbed. David, the woman's not well."

"She's an artist, for god's sake!"

"Maybe you're right." Tolbert shook his head sadly. "But I'd hate to see you plant a time bomb in your future."

21 / SHAKESPEARE NUT

The Mighty Hamlet? David knew he owed the nickname to his father. He smiled to think that whenever he remembered the old days in Ste. Thérèse, he'd find himself a bit player in an extravaganza that starred the old man: spontaneous, excessive — larger than life. Back came a particular Sunday afternoon.

"Nothing to do?" his father bounced up out of his arm chair. David had been moping around the house, complaining of boredom. "By jingo, I'll give you something to do!"

Hitching up his baggy trousers, tightening the necktie that served as a belt, he made for the front porch.

"Not again, Gerard." David's mother, working in the kitchen, put down her iron. "You're not digging out Shakespeare?"

His father waved her off and kept going. David could hear him rummaging around, knocking over lamps and useless doodads he refused to discard because sooner or later the next Depression would hit and then what?

After a while, he returned with half a dozen dog-eared paperbacks. He sat down on the couch and hauled David down beside him. "Here, you son of a gun!" He sorted the paperbacks, reading off their titles. "*Midsummer Night's Dream, Merchant of Venice, The Tempest, Othello* — there you go! Have you read *Othello?*"

"Gerard, he's only fourteen."

"Okay, look — *The Taming of the Shrew*. Or what about *Romeo and Juliet!* Start with that."

"Dad, I've read that one, remember?"

"Okay, what about *Macbeth?*

"Haven't you got anything, I don't know... more contemporary?"

"More contemporary? What could be more contemporary than jealousy and manipulation? Or ambition and murder? Or revenge? Never mind. Why not go straight to *Hamlet*, the greatest story ever told." His father jumped up and began pacing, declaiming from memory: "To be or not to be, that is the question...."

"Gerard, for god's sake."

"What a sense of language!" He thrust *Hamlet* at David. "Here! Take the mighty Bard and read! And don't tell me you've got nothing to do."

That was the father David adored. The histrionic Shakespeare nut. The would-be actor. Though by 1963, he realized now, his father had quit making amateur movies. The summer before, even, he and Uncle Alphonse had worked on a war picture using miniatures. Every Sunday, they'd commandeer the back yard and scramble around a plastic swimming pool with a camera, blowing up toy ships with firecrackers.

They never finished the picture. Just ran out of gas, his father said later, when David asked. All those extra hours he put in at *La Victoire.* As the only reporter who spoke English, he'd work most Friday nights and some Saturdays. Needed Sundays to recover.

Sometimes, David remembered, his father would complain that nothing big ever happened on the North Shore. He'd slam *The Chronicle* on the kitchen table and shout that he could do a better job than half those hot-shot reporters downtown.

Still, his father was never happier, David thought, than when he worked for *La Victoire.* He loved the public profile, the recognition that went with the job: "There goes Nelligan. Wonder what he's working on?"

If he missed downtown Montreal, the hubbub and hurly-burly, he was glad at least that he didn't spend ninety minutes each day commuting by train. "Do you know what that adds up to?" he'd ask. "Four hundred and fifty minutes a week. Seven and a half hours."

Once a month or so, David's father would go drinking with the boys, either in Bonaventure — someone would drive him home to Ste-Thérèse — or else at *La Fin Du Monde,* the hotel at the top of the street.

When he drank, he became somebody else. He'd sit on the couch and brood, listen to his jazz records, old seventy-eights made of glass: Duke Ellington, Artie Shaw, Dizzy Gillespie. Sometimes he'd pace the kitchen floor muttering about his boss, a man named Grenier. Other times, he'd bang and slam around, shouting that it was a jungle out there, a rat-race, but the fix was in. A guy with his abilities should be working, not at a small-town rag where they didn't appreciate him, but at *The Chronicle* or *The Montreal Standard.*

Those nights, when David's mother called from their bedroom, told him to come to bed, he'd refuse, answer that he wasn't coming to bed tonight. In the morning, when David got up to deliver *Chronicles,* there he'd be on the couch, covered in an old bedspread.

One night, must have been after eleven, his father brought home a friend. They sat talking and drinking beer at the kitchen table. From his bed, David could hear every word. He deduced that the visitor was a policeman named Fraticelli, the only English cop at the station in Bonaventure. In his spare time, he learned now, Fraticelli wrote detective stories. He'd just had one published in a magazine.

David's father had gone out into the front porch and dug out his box of old stories, pieces he'd written during his Air Force days. He read one of them aloud, a funny story David hadn't heard before about a soldier on latrine duty who borrows a jeep to visit a girl friend — and never arrives.

Fraticelli, who had a big, booming voice, laughed and shouted: "That's publishable, Gerard! What else you got there?"

David's father took out some columns he'd written a few months before, humorous first-person sketches that Grenier had refused to publish. He read one about visiting Blue Bonnets Raceway, losing money on the horses. Fraticelli pounded the table.

"Gerard, keep the noise down!" David's mother cried from bed. "People have to get up in the morning."

His father read another unpublished sketch, this one about trying to sell a house during the spring flood. Fraticelli laughed until he cried. Then he said: "Grenier refused to publish this stuff?"

"He told me readers didn't want it."

"He didn't want you showing him up, that's all. You should do something with these pieces."

From bed, his mother called: "Gerard, can I see you a moment."

David's father pushed back his chair and went into his bedroom. After a moment, when he returned to the kitchen, Fraticelli said: "Gerry, it's getting late. I'd better be on my way."

"No, no," his father said. "No rush."

But even David could tell his father was just being polite. At the door, Fraticelli said: "Forget Grenier, Gerry. Write some more of those sketches. Get a collection together and send them out."

"You're right. Yes, I'll do that."

But he never did.

22 / OUZO IN THE FACE

"No secession from Canada without referendum, says Quebec's new leader." The headline blares from a yellowing copy of *The Athens News* dated November 18, 1976. I remember buying the newspaper in the port city of Palamedes, at a kiosk near the bus depot. Standing there and reading that René Lévesque had led the separatist Parti Québécois to its first election victory.

Once we'd recovered from the shock of the news, Isabelle and I disagreed about what it meant. She claimed the separatist victory made independence inevitable.

"Nonsense," I responded. "Federalist parties took fifty-nine per cent of the popular vote."

"It's the beginning of the end, David."

"Shouldn't we wait for the referendum? It says here that Quebecers were simply voting for a change of government."

"Vive le Québec libre!"

Realizing where this would take us, we decided to go our separate ways for a couple of hours. We'd come to Palamedes for a respite. Back in Apolakia, angry words had become the norm. Shouting matches, ugly gestures.

Since arriving in Greece, Isabelle had become more temperamental than ever. This always happened, she said, when she wrote a first draft. Also, she blamed our physical circumstances. In the kitchen, instead of a stove, we had a hot plate. But no refrigerator. No hot water. No space. We kept knocking pots and pans onto the floor. All of which bothered Isabelle more than me.

In the bathroom, she noted, we had no tub, just a cold water shower and a seatless toilet. That, at least, was clean, because I went at it weekly with Greece's answer to Ajax.

Otherwise, neither of us did much cleaning.

I willed myself to ignore the conditions. Isabelle tried but felt angry. "My writing is just as important as yours," she said one evening, "though you deliberately undermine me with your attitude."

We were elbow to elbow in the tiny kitchen, cooking supper: "My attitude?"

"You try to make me feel guilty for not waiting on you hand and foot — for not fulfilling the traditional female role."

"Isabelle, you're projecting."

"No, I'm not. You've set Arianna up as this paragon of virtue. You're always secretly comparing. You think she's perfect."

"Here we go again."

"Tu ne comprends rien, David. I feel empathy for Arianna. It's you I'm criticizing." She unwrapped a dozen small fish. "You and I were going to visit Athens — the two of us together."

"That's when I was leaving Greece *before* Christmas."

"You think I don't want to visit the Parthenon? We're working seven days a week, no sightseeing. All I do is cook your dinners and take out the garbage."

"I've been carrying the load around here, Isabelle, and you know it."

"But sightseeing, honest-to-goodness touristing, that you're going to do with Arianna."

"If you're so desperate to go to Athens at Christmas, we could have stuck with the original plan. But no. That wasn't good enough."

"You're selfish, David."

"You wanted me to remain beyond Christmas. You agreed that I'd meet Arianna in Athens. Now I'm meeting her alone and that's that."

"Selfish, selfish, selfish!"

I turned on my heel and strode to my study.

Half an hour later, when she called me for supper, all sweetness and light, I apologized for walking off and Isabelle smiled brightly: "That's okay, David. I just hope you can take a joke."

"Come again?"

"*Voila!* Food fit for mortals." She whipped a tea towel off the plate in front of me. It was piled high with bloody fish heads. Garnished with fish guts. "What's the matter, David? Eat up."

Staring at this meal from hell, I realized just how mobile I was. One rucksack, one suitcase, one typewriter. Back in my study, eating a peanut butter sandwich, I looked around at what I'd have to pack. Thought again of my work-in-progress. I had to finish the rewrite here in Callisto or I might lose it. Isabelle had convinced me of that. Besides, Arianna had already bought her plane ticket.

I willed myself to forget the fish heads and awoke next morning with a new proposal. Why didn't we visit the port city of Palamedes? Take two days and stay overnight in a hotel. See the city, shop for Christmas, maybe visit some nearby ruins.

Isabelle wasn't hard to convince.

We rode the bus up island and rented a double room, with shower, in the Hotel Theseus. Ten dollars a night included breakfast. We couldn't stop marvelling. First afternoon, having agreed to disagree about the Quebec election, we did some Christmas shopping. Later, we splurged on dinner: our old favorite, lamb souvla. Agreed we'd done well to take this holiday.

Next morning, though, we had a second go-round about the election. Then, while touring some ruins, we argued about when, exactly, I'd leave Greece: before my birthday or after. Disagreed about what, exactly, we'd already agreed.

Still, towards the end of that second afternoon, as we sat drinking ouzo at an outdoor café, watching motorized three-wheelers raise dust in the streets, we agreed the trip had been a success. Isabelle said she hoped we'd share many more such afternoons. I'd lived with her for over a year, and so she understood that I needed time alone with Arianna. But maybe next summer? After visiting the cottage in Kenya? Maybe we could all three rent a house in Wajadili?

Fat chance Arianna would go for that, I thought. But I didn't want to get into it, and said simply: "Let's see how Christmas goes."

"Sometimes I think you and Arianna should disappear somewhere and start a family," she said. "That's what Arianna wants, really. Maybe you, too."

Isabelle was uncanny. I remembered fantasizing, in recent a letter to Arianna, about settling in the Eastern Townships, opening a bookstore, raising a family. But I said, "I think you're wrong."

"I'm not wrong." Isabelle smiled brightly. "But tell me something, David. What would you say to having a child with me?" She must have read alarm in my face. "No, I'm not pregnant. I'm speaking hypothetically."

"I don't know what I'd say. I'd have to discuss it with Arianna."

"Discuss it with Arianna? What's she got to do with it?" Isabelle jumped to her feet. "You're living with me, remember?"

She threw her ouzo in my face, spun on her heel and marched off towards the bus depot. More stunned than angry, I wiped my face with a napkin and paid the bill. It was supernatural, almost scary, the way Isabelle could ferret out my secret thoughts. As I made for the bus depot, I thought: Maybe, just maybe, she really *is* psychic.

23 / ARIANNA SPOTS PUPPETRY

Flash back just over a year, to that intellectual honeymoon in Ste-Adele. Summertime, 1975. Having worked all morning, typing away madly in the shed behind Isabelle's cabin, David would go jogging in the afternoon, trotting along the winding dirt roads that ringed the nearby lake. For exercise, he said. But really he needed to find a quiet spot in the woods where he could sit and weep. The new sex was good, all right — but he missed Arianna. He'd begun to wonder whether, in leaving her, he hadn't made the biggest mistake of his life.

On returning from his run, David would withdraw into the writing shed to drink red wine (insulation) and pound out point-form missives explaining why, come September, he should, after all, move into an apartment of his own. Unable, as yet, to tell the simple truth — "Isabelle, I admire you but I don't love you, I was wrong to leave Arianna" — he focused on Isabelle's nationalist friends.

Jacques Bienvenue and half a dozen others had arrived unannounced one Saturday afternoon. They'd brought two cases of beer, and halfway through the evening, inevitably, they'd begun debating the merits of sovereignty-association — whether Quebec should declare independence outright or move towards it slowly.

David said: "What about Canada?"

"Canada?" Jacques Bienvenue did an extravagant double-take. "Canada does not exist."

"Canada's a nightmare," Isabelle said, "from which we're trying to awake."

"No, seriously," David said. "Isn't there something to be said for the idea of a multi-national state?"

"Trudeau!" Bienvenue roared. "You've been reading that goddamn sell-out!"

The room erupted in a chorus of boos.

Someone said: "Two scorpions in a bottle."

Bienvenue said: "Oh, English. You're priceless. What's your name again?"

David looked around the room but nobody would meet his eye — not even Isabelle. He said: "Yeah, well, I think I'll go for a walk." Discussion resumed as he went out the front door.

An hour later, when he returned, the party was winding down. He went into the back room and lay on a cot, reading, until everybody had left. Later, Isabelle told him he'd taken the politics too personally.

This might be true, David admitted in one of his point-form missives. Fact remained: her friends didn't want him around — they'd made that clear. To them, he was an interloper. Their living together would never work. Better he should get his own apartment.

Isabelle recognized this as a smokescreen, if only because, night after night, David would drink too much wine and end up weeping in her arms, wondering what he'd done. She'd stroke his head. Give her friends time, she said, and they'd see what she saw: *un de nous-autres.* The problem was that he and Arianna had been too exclusive for too long. Sure, they'd been happy. But happiness wasn't the point.

Their claustrophobic relationship had stunted their growth as human beings. Returning to Arianna would destroy him as a writer. He needed broader experience. Anyway, he'd committed himself. He couldn't back out now. It was too late for Isabelle to find someone else to move into the house, and alone she couldn't manage the mortgage payments. He was honor-bound.

In mid-July, when he met Arianna in Montreal, David hid his anguish. He'd come into the city to chase down a grad-student fellowship. Arianna was leaving town for a month, taking the Volkswagen, and they had to discuss giving notice on their Aylmer Street flat. They met at that "dinky little apartment," so full of memories, and, over coffee, sorted out their business.

They moved from the kitchen table to the living room. David said they'd been "pathetically honest" with each other, always revealing everything, and maybe this had constrained them both. Arianna said, "Maybe."

David began paraphrasing Isabelle. The idea of life-long commitment was out-moded, he said, the institution of marriage, dead. He and Arianna had grown larger through loving one another, but they'd leaned on one another too much, allowed certain capacities to atrophy. "I'm a stumblebum in the kitchen."

"And I can't do my income tax? That's reason to walk out on a marriage? David, get serious."

"The other day I thought of Thomas Wolfe." Now he was pacing. "I could never understand why he parted company with his editor, Maxwell Perkins, who was also his dearest friend. Wolfe tried to explain that it had to do with his need, as a writer, to keep growing." He stopped pacing. "I think I understand that now."

"Give me a break, David." Arianna stood up. "If you were seeking freedom and growth, you'd be getting your own place. Not moving into someone else's."

"I made a commitment to Isabelle."

"You made a prior commitment to me. We got married, remember?"

"Marriage doesn't last forever."

"Want to know the truth, David? She's jerking you around like a puppet."

"Nobody's jerking me around. It's combustion. Put certain chemicals together and boom!"

Arianna started fishing around in her purse.

"Isabelle makes all the right feminist noises," she said. "Sister this, sister that. But when she wants a man, even if he's still just a boy, then sister, look out."

"In other circumstances, Isabelle says, you two might have been best of friends."

"Isabelle says this, Isabelle says that." Out of her purse she pulled her wedding ring and flung it in his face. "Damn you for a pathetic fool!"

To his astonishment, then, Arianna burst into tears and came at him flailing. She was lithe and athletic and landed a couple of blows before he grabbed her wrists and hung on.

After a few seconds, she stopped struggling and said, "Let me go!"

David knelt and retrieved her wedding ring — a ring they'd bought together in England. He offered it to her, but Arianna slapped it away and said, "Give it to that two-faced bitch!"

She wheeled and walked out the door.

24 / A BRIEF HISTORY
OF QUEBEC NATIONALISM

Fourteen years later, in that cold, empty house on Old Orchard Avenue, David Nelligan glanced at his watch. Seven minutes past eleven. He'd missed the top of the news. He hurried to the family room anyway, turned on the television and sat back with his clicker. Montrealers, he learned, had begun digging out after the worst blizzard of the year. Click. Three people had died in a car accident on *Pont Victoria*. Click. Click.

Wait, what was this? Believe it: a documentary profile of Paul Rose, ex-terrorist. One of the FLQ guys who, in October of 1970, had murdered cabinet minister Pierre Laporte. More recently, Rose had denounced the Supreme Court ruling that shot down the language law, Bill 101. Now, the announcer said, the man was becoming a folk hero. Cut to a rally in the north end: Rose addressing students at a community college.

When he'd finished speaking, David knew, two hundred people had descended on a nearby bakery, chanting *"Le Québec aux Québécois!"* They'd plastered the store with stickers. Reason? A bilingual sign in the front window. Big Brother was watching, *mon ami*. Out of habit, David picked up a notepad and scrawled, "Get clippings on Paul Rose."

He resumed channel surfing. No mention anywhere of the notorious Nelligan or his infamous campaign — a small mercy. Though maybe he'd missed it? The only other item of interest came courtesy of the nationalist St-Jean Baptiste Society, which had published a study demonstrating that the so-called Anglo Exodus was just part of a North American trend. David said, "Yeah, right."

Back in the living room, he found the file marked "Calypso 101." He dropped his Paul-Rose note into it, then stood flipping through old jottings and newspaper clippings. Remembering. Once he'd removed the bilingual sign, vandals had confined themselves to scrawling grafitti on the front window. And the bookstore did well enough that by 1985, when Tolbert decided he'd had enough of working two full-time jobs, David and Arianna bought him out.

With two pre-schoolers at home, Arianna decided to focus on care-giving — refused to apologize for it — and David ran the bookstore. He watched, baffled and frustrated, as English-speaking Quebecers left the province by the tens of thousands. Those who remained overflowed into language classes and camped out overnight to get their children into French immersion, but no matter. Nationalist firebrands still went around declaring that the real enemy of a French Quebec was *"la minorité anglaise."*

David attended a meeting of Alliance Quebec. Led by lawyers, this English-rights group was mounting legal challenges to Bill 101, notably those clauses banning English from commercial signs. David remembered an articulate young woman speaking from the floor. She said non-francophones made up eighteen per cent of the Quebec population but only one per cent of civil servants: "What does that tell you?"

The lawyers responded that this imbalance had many causes. Let's not be inflammatory, they said. Experience had shown that militancy made matters worse.

The young woman said, "What do you mean, 'worse?' Worse than FLQ firebombings? Worse than kidnapping and murdering cabinet ministers?"

Ancient history, the lawyers said. They had an unbeatable case against Bill 101. They couldn't lose. David smiled grimly. Over the next couple of years, the lawyers had proved right. Court after court ruled that Quebec's sign-language provisions discriminated against English-speakers. Finally, a couple of months back, the Supreme Court of Canada stated the obvious: Quebec's ban on English-language signs was discriminatory and unconstitutional.

December, 1988. English speakers rejoiced — but too soon. Despite promises and reassurances, and against the advice of all four of his Anglophone cabinet ministers — three of whom promptly resigned — the Quebec premier invoked a little known "notwithstanding clause" in the Canadian constitution.

Notwithstanding the Charter of Rights and Freedoms, English-language signs were banned from the streets of Quebec. So said Bill

178. Indoors, English could appear on signs — as long as French was clearly predominant. Bigger letters. Brighter colours. Whatever.

Yet even this "inside-outside solution" failed to satisfy the nationalists. They organized a protest parade in Montreal, the largest in twenty years. More than sixty thousand people hit the streets to demand the return of Bill 101 and the removal of English signs of any kind. They chanted and waved flags and placards saying *"Le Québec aux Québécois"* and *"101 ou 401"*: *If you don't like it here, blockhead, hit the highway to Toronto.*

The day of the parade, David was walking along Sherbrooke Street, lugging a box of books to the post office, when the marchers arrived in force. One of the organizers was strutting along with a megaphone, crying: "Give us back our unilingual signs! We want nothing but French in our stores and businesses, inside as well as outside! Nothing but French!"

That's when David realized what he was seeing: the face of ethnic nationalism. The hair on the back of his neck stood up, and suddenly he heard himself shout: "Wake up! You're sleep-walking!"

He found himself hurrying along beside the marchers, lugging his box of books and shouting in French: "Wake up! You're committing suicide."

For a while, lost in their chanting, the marchers didn't even see him. Finally, a burly man with a beard stepped out of the crowd and slammed him up against a parked car: *"Ferme ta guele, mon hostie d'Anglais."*

David shut his face. But he knew then, even before the burly man spit on the ground and rejoined his fellows, that he could remain silent no longer. No matter the cost, he had to speak out.

25 /

THE COURAGE OF EMMANUEL TOLBERT

Now, in west-end Montreal, the nationalist marchers brought back the first time he'd been singled out as *un hostie d'Anglais* — which was also the night Emmanuel Tolbert covered himself in glory. But take it from the *Salle de danse,* recognized among north-shore teenagers of the early nineteen sixties as the centre of the universe. It was a glorified hotdog stand, really, created out of an old meeting hall near the centre of town, where the train bridge crossed the highway.

The *Salle de danse* attracted teenagers from thirty miles around, even from Montreal and the distant South Shore, friends of friends out for a drive in a borrowed car and needing somewhere to go. Seven nights a week the dance hall was jumping with older teenagers, but weekends were especially wild, and out front you'd see scooters and motorbikes and top-down Lincoln convertibles with pretty girls lounging against them.

The dance hall boasted a standing-room-only counter where you could shout orders for hotdogs, hamburgers and patates frites, with a couple of short-order cooks behind it, muscular guys who doubled as bouncers and wore white shirts with sleeves rolled up to their shoulders. Also an arcade area with half a dozen pinball machines, one of which rewarded winners by spitting nickels, usually three or six at a time, but sometimes forty or fifty, a major event.

The dance hall proper you entered via the arcade or else off the highway through big double doors that stood open. You stepped up into a barn-like area with a hardwood floor and a high ceiling, nothing but rafters to the roof. Wooden benches lined the walls, and in one corner stood a giant Wurlitzer that was hooked up to loudspeakers and blasted rock'n'roll for half a mile.

Until he was twelve or thirteen, David adopted his parents' attitude towards the *Salle de danse* — wanted nothing to do with the place. Then came a summer, must have been 1962, when he recognized its attraction. One evening, out riding bicycles with a friend named Michel Thibideau, and drawn by the blaring of a favorite Elvis Presley song, he suggested they park their bicycles and look inside.

Pretty girls in short-shorts and tight sweaters were dancing together, laughing and whirling around the floor. Most of the guys were playing pinball or just watching, though occasionally one of them ventured to dance. This wasn't so bad, after all, and David and Thibideau not only stayed, drinking cokes, but returned the next night and the night after that.

The only problem with the *Salle de danse* was that most of the regulars who hung out there were the sons and daughters of summer people from Montreal. The teenage boys were veterans of the French-English gang wars that raged in the city all winter, especially in districts like Park Extension, Point St-Charles and St-Henri.

To David, their attitude was new. Children in Ste-Thérèse, whether French or English, had always got along. In summer, they'd spend hours together at the crossroads, playing Red Light, Hide and Seek or Mother May I Take A Step. In winter, they'd tobaggon at the Sand Hills, just north of the tracks, or lace on skates and play tag or hockey on the frozen lake.

David thought of himself as half-French. His father was precisely that, his mother had Acadian ancestors, and he himself spoke mostly French with three of his best friends: Thibideau, Bergeron and Bolduc. All three lived south of the highway, *Chemin d'Oka*, either on *Avenue des Oracles*, as he did, or one street over on *Avenue des Archanges*. Of the three only Thibideau spoke any English at all. His dead father had been an American, but his mother sent him and all of his siblings to the French school half a mile up the highway.

The local French kids also included a couple of girls, friends of his sister Janey, and a guy named Caouette, a foster child they all thought of as crazy — *"y'est fou, lui"* — and who wasn't crazy at all, David realized later, but emotionally disturbed. He lived three houses down. Every couple of weeks his foster father, an overweight policeman, would take Crazy Caouette out into their garage and beat him with a belt. You'd hear him howling up and down the street and know he'd been caught masturbating.

The English-speaking contingent included Bobby Middleton, who walked with a limp and swung one arm stiff and awkward across his chest, the result of childhood polio; and Brian Wiggins, a chubby, sandy-haired boy whose ex-Yorkshireman father, a roaring tyrant, worked nights at the Canadair plant in Cartierville. Then there was Emmanuel Tolbert, who'd recently immigrated from Trinidad with his older brother, a school teacher.

Tolbert lived west up the highway in Pointe Calumet, two or three miles away, and turned up one morning on the yellow school bus that David rode to Bonaventure. Soon the boys were visiting back and forth by bicycle. They'd shoot baskets — both of them basketball nuts — or walk their dogs in the woods. Tolbert, too, felt the attraction of the *Salle de danse* — "this is more like it!" — and overnight became more of a fixture in Ste-Thérèse than most of the guys who lived there.

The summer of 1962 brought French-English incidents — a *"maudit Anglais"* here, a "French Pea Soup" there. Three French guys caught Wiggins alone at the beach and slapped his face until he cried. Half a dozen others chased a newcomer, a quiet boy named Austin who lived for his stamp collection, all the way down *Avenue des Cherubins* to the lake. He escaped only by plunging through a filthy ditch, waist-deep.

From this harassment David enjoyed a fragile immunity. Several boys had eyed him suspiciously after hearing him speak English with Tolbert. But they'd also heard him talk French with Thibideau, and so made no move.

Soon David was visiting the dance hall every night, sometimes with Bolduc or Thibideau, sometimes with Tolbert, sometimes even alone. He'd noticed that one older guy — Raymond Larose, must have been all of sixteen — had girls swarming all over him. He was tall and blonde and not bad-looking, but he owed his popularity, David decided, to the way he danced — with grace and effortless authority.

David resolved to learn how to dance like Raymond Larose, and for hours he'd stand by the pinball machines and watch Larose weave and glide around the floor, memorizing his moves. Next day, at home, he'd practice Larose's steps and even his gestures, first alone and then with his sister Janey.

A desire to check one of Larose's fanciest moves, a double-time shuffle he'd almost mastered, seized David one evening as he walked along the highway with Middleton, Wiggins, Tolbert and two or three other guys, all of them English, as it happened, except Crazy Caouette. They'd been playing scrub baseball in a field beside the train tracks — Thibideau had left early, summoned by his mother — and as they approached the dance hall on their way home, with Elvis Presley belting out Hound Dog, David suggested they stop.

Wiggins didn't like the idea but Tolbert was keen and David insisted: "The music's in English, isn't it?"

Raymond Larose was on the dance floor, whirling two girls at once. This was new. Wiggins said, "Okay, David, you've looked. Let's get out of here."

"Relax. What's the hurry?"

David remained by the door, enthralled, telling Tolbert: "See that double-time shuffle? That's what I'm after."

Wiggins tugged at his sleeve and gestured. Over by the pinball machines, two French guys were moving from group to group, talking and nodding in their direction. David agreed it was time to leave.

The ballplayers walked east along the highway.

"Don't look now," Wiggins said, "but we're not alone."

Twenty-five or thirty French guys had left the dance hall and were following them along the highway. David counted seven ballplayers, including himself. Normally, a couple of the guys would have turned south right away, down *Avenues des Cherubins,* but David said: "Let's stick together. Head for my house. And whatever you do, don't run."

As the boys turned south off the highway onto *Avenue des Oracles,* stones started whizzing overhead. Thrown high, they weren't meant to strike anybody. But one stone hit Crazy Caouette in the shoulder. He panicked, broke into a trot and raced down the street yelling, not in his native French but in broken English: "My daddy policeman! My daddy policeman! I get my daddy!"

Behind David and his friends, thirty French guys started to run. Crazy Caouette escaped, but the rest of the boys soon stood surrounded in the middle of *Avenue des Oracles*.

"Qu'est que c'est, ca?" David asked. "What's all this?"

"On va te casser la gueule, mon hostie," one of the tougher-looking guys answered. "We're going to punch your face in."

"Pourquoi? On n'a rien fait. We haven't done anything."

"Toi, t'es correct. Mes les autres sont têtes carrées. Maudits Anglais. You, you're all right. But these guys are god-damned English blockheads."

David found Raymond Larose in the crowd and addressed him. *"C'est de bonne guerre, ça?* Thirty against six?"

The biggest, meanest-looking of the French guys, all bent nose and sinewy arms, stepped forward and shoved David in the chest: *"Ferme ta gueule, mon hostie d'Anglais. Tu parles francais, mais t'es quand-même une tête-carrée."*

Larose grabbed the guy's arm. *"Y'a raison, Ti 'Ris. Il faut se battre à un contre un."*

Tolbert said, "What's he saying?"

"Pourquoi faut-il se battre?" David said. "What have we done to you?"

"Un contre un!" The cry went up around the circle. *"Un contre un!"*

"Bon, d'accord," David said, his mouth dry.

Wiggins said, "David, have you lost your mind? This guy'll kill you."

"One against one," Tolbert said. "I get it."

He put his hand on David's shoulder. "Stand aside, buddy. This guy's mine."

Knowing that Tolbert stood a better chance of surviving, David did as his friend asked — and not without relief. Tolbert began dancing around in front of Ti 'Ris with his fists raised. He was big for fourteen, and his brother had taught him a few moves, but this French boy was snarling and street-wise and at least three years older.

Still, Ti 'Ris swung and missed. Tolbert hit him in the face, once, twice. Clearly, he was the better boxer. Every time Ti 'Ris swung, Tolbert danced out of range. He landed three unanswered punches to the body and one more to the head. Enraged, Ti 'Ris rushed him, taking two shots in the face, and tackled him like a football player.

David leapt forward but three guys grabbed his arms. Ti 'Ris straddled Tolbert, started slapping his face back and forth. Larose and a couple of other French guys tried to pull him off: *"Assez, Ti 'Ris. Assez!"*

"Tabernaque! La police!"

Crazy Caouette was running up the street towards them, yelling: "My daddy coming! My daddy coming!"

Behind him, his step-father was backing his police car out of the driveway. Ti 'Ris jumped off Tolbert and thirty guys scattered, jumping hedges and fences, leaping ditches. They were gone before Crazy Caouette's father pulled up and rolled down his window: *"Ça va, les gars?"*

"Pas'd problème," David said. After a moment the policeman drove slowly up the street, looking this way and that, establishing his presence. By now Tolbert was on his feet, bleeding from the mouth. His left eye was puffy and he was struggling to keep from crying. "I had him beat, did you see? The bastard jumped me. I had him beat."

Brian Wiggins said, "Fucking frogs."

Then, remembering, he glanced over at David.

"Ignorant bastards," David said. "Ignorant city bastards."

26 / CRY FROM THE HEART

Cut to that "dinky little apartment" on Aylmer Street, summer of 1975: David showered, changed his jeans and put on his favorite checkered workshirt. He left the top two buttons undone, the way Isabelle liked. He was roasting a chicken, the fanciest meal he could prepare, when she arrived from Ste-Adele. She'd washed and blow-dried her hair, which hung black and loose to her shoulders. She wore a wrap-around print skirt she'd bought in Ecuador, all reds and blues and golds.

As they sat drinking chilled white wine, waiting for the chicken to roast, Isabelle said: "David, what's wrong? You're a bundle of nerves."

Two days before, David had returned to the apartment from rambling the streets to find a letter waiting. Arianna wrote from Timmins, Ontario, where she was staying not with her mother but with friends who owned a house on the outskirts. She was living in a big tent on their property and working nights as a waitress and barmaid. She was sorry for the way she'd behaved, she wrote. She didn't hate Isabelle, as he believed, but felt numb when she thought of her — and simply could not respect her as a woman.

Her anger and bitterness are frightening, David. To tell the truth, I think she needs psychological help. I don't know why you can't see her clearly. I only hope you never get in her way. Isabelle will stop at nothing to achieve her ends. Nothing. These are harsh words but truth is often harsh, as I've recently discovered.

I admit that I am having a hard time right now. Some day when I understand it better, I will be able to look at it more objectively. Five years together is a long time, and a long time is hard to forget in a short time. Actually, I doubt if I will ever forget it. I doubt that I'll want to.

This fall, I'll continue my studies at Université de Montréal. Finish the program next spring. Then, who knows? I'd like to work abroad if I can. I'd like to travel, to get inside another country's art and culture. I'd hoped to do this with you, but I see now that was a fantasy.

I know you will think me silly, but one of the hardest parts for me is the mental picture I have of you and Isabelle in bed together. Those were my most precious times with you — having a bad dream and waking up to you. Waking up in the morning in your arms. Just loving you. Nobody will ever replace you, David. How I loved you — and still love you. Damn it. If I didn't love you, all this would be easy.

Anyway, I've started looking into getting a divorce. We don't have any kids so it shouldn't be too difficult. Maybe we can do it without lawyers. I do love you, David, but I don't want to hang onto you as I did at first. Thank you for all the good times....

When he'd finished reading, David stumbled into the bedroom, the one he'd shared with Arianna, and fell across the bed. Buried his face in the pillow.

Next day, when he sat down to reply, David had been away from Isabelle for almost a week. But still he couldn't think straight, and his feelings made him dream:

Arianna, I love you and miss you. I never wanted you out of my life and don't want you out now. It's far too early to talk about divorce. I still think the solution is for the three of us to live in the Outremont house come fall. Three separate rooms. Get away from the couply stuff D.H. Lawrence railed against. I think of Carl and Emma Jung and Toni Wolff. Somehow, they made it work.

I could share different activities with each of you. You two could go places together. Each of us could have other relationships. Unconventional, certainly, but maybe not insane. We could really try to share. Isabelle would have to agree, of course. And the three of us would have to work out details...

I haven't shown Isabelle this letter, but I'll make a photocopy. I'll show it to her after I've heard from you. That's the kind of openness we'll need, honesty cutting three ways instead of two. Any other arrangement would be destructive to all of us. I know both of you. I think you could learn to love each other. Please write soon....

Now, when Isabelle asked what was wrong, David said: "I need your help, Isabelle." That much he'd rehearsed. "Yesterday, in a moment of weakness, I sent Arianna a letter. Now I think I made a mistake. But maybe not."

"What are you talking about?"

"I reasoned that passion doesn't last forever." He handed Isabelle a copy of the letter he'd sent Arianna. "What happens when it wanes?"

Sitting on the tatty couch, Isabelle read the letter once, then read it again. She grew red in the face. When she looked up, David said: "We've both tried straight marriages and seen them fail. Maybe we should try something else? The society we live in wants everybody in couples. But to hell with society. Think of Sartre and de Beauvoir."

"My God, you're a blockhead." Isabelle was on her feet. "What you're really afraid of, David, is that I won't be able to meet all your demands. That I've got too much going on in my life."

Unable to face the simple truth — that he wanted to return to Arianna — David said: "You do spend a lot of time with your nationalist friends."

"I also want to be loved, David." Now Isabelle was pacing, fighting to regain control. "I want to be loved passionately, intensely, wholeheartedly. I'm ready to make a commitment. And you aren't. I understand that — but why would I pursue such an unbalanced relationship?"

"How unbalanced? We'd all three live as we pleased."

"You'd never be able to handle it, David. You're the most possessive man I know."

"You're the possessive one, Isabelle. But maybe we could try a veto system? That letter was a cry from the heart."

"Yes, it was — but not to me."

"I keep thinking, 'What have I done to Arianna?'"

"What have you done to Arianna? Oh, David."

She sat down beside him on the couch, began running her fingers through his hair. "You spent five years with her in an exclusive relationship. Five years exploring each other, free together, travelling the world. You didn't tell her you never loved her. That she was sick and needed help. You told her you wanted to explore in new directions."

Isabelle had opened his shirt to slide her hand over his bare chest. "Arianna is free of commitments. Maybe you're jealous of that. You prefer to see her as victim. Of course, she loves you. You're very lovable, David. But you use that to get your own way. You hurt me all the time, yet you're so unaware of it."

Isabelle began working at his belt buckle.

Afterwards, as they wolfed down chicken, they talked literature, tacitly postponing more emotional topics. A few days later, when David received a reply from Arianna, further discussion became academic.

That was the first time in a long time, David, that I've heard you expressing your own feelings about what happened, not someone else's. But you blame yourself too much. It happened and that's all. Yes, it is too simplistic to blame Isabelle for everything. I don't blame her for the separation — though I can't help blaming her for the way it happened. It happened so much the way her own separation did, and we were never Isabelle and Kurt.

Yes, we married young, and maybe we didn't experience enough separately. Maybe this split-up is best for both of us. I'm glad if you're happy with Isabelle. Truly, I want you to be happy. I do miss you and love you. Nothing can change that. I do know, however, that the three of us, you and me and Isabelle, can't live in the same house. It simply would not work. I plan to find my own apartment....

27 / CALYPSO 101

Now, in the house on Old Orchard, David Nelligan flipped through a file folder and stopped at a color photo of himself standing on a step ladder in front of the bookstore, hammer in hand. He was pretending to nail up the bilingual sign he'd removed years before: *Librairie Calypso Canada / Calypso Canada Books.* In fact, he'd already nailed up the sign, but the photographer from *The Chronicle* had wanted a single shot that told the story.

The reporter was less sympathetic, he remembered. She preferred David's previous position: Why rock the boat? But she was professional and painstaking, and she'd obviously perused his mimeographed sheet, which doubled as a poster. David admired her technique. Begin slowly, establish a rapport: "You say here in your sheet that Francophone schools have taught pernicious myths about English-speakers."

"They've created this stereotype of Anglos as wealthy Westmounters. You know: we're all fat-cat exploiters descended from the original conquerers. It's ludicrous, really. Most so-called Anglos have working-class backgrounds. And only a quarter of us stem from British stock. We've got to stop feeling guilty."

"What do you think of the 'distinct society?'"

"Code words for the Quebec project. Of course Quebec is distinct. And I love the French language and culture. I'm part-French myself."

"Do I hear a 'but' in your tone?"

"If you like. I'm no longer prepared to accept discrimination and something close to racism for the sake of creating a unilingual French Quebec. An ethnic state."

"Strong words."

"Have you seen the marchers in the streets? Heard them chanting *'Le Québec aux Québécois'*? This is a society with a mission. And that mission excludes me."

"The marchers want to protect the French language."

"That's the cover story. They see English as an obscenity on the social landscape and want Anglos to get the hell out. Oh, English-speakers can remain, all right. As long as we're willing to become second-class citizens, silent and invisible — the new white niggers of North America."

The reporter scribbled furiously.

"Actually, there's a third choice," David said. "Join Calypso 101."

"Okay, why this campaign of civil disobedience?"

"Because the strictly legal approach doesn't work. Bill 178 has taught us that. If you play by the rules and win, they'll simply change the rules."

"What about that new Anglo-rights group?"

"The English Front? They're potentially violent. Maybe it's the Canadian in me, but I prefer to take a peaceful approach."

"Can you be more specific?"

"Start with the sign provisions. I think stores should post bilingual signs. That business people and merchants should go to jail if necessary."

"Bookstores are exempt, right? So personally, you aren't in any danger."

"Not legally speaking, no."

"You call your campaign Calypso 101. A little publicity for the bookstore?"

"I had to give it a name."

The reporter flipped her notebook shut. As she stood, she said: "Any society has its extreme elements. Aren't you afraid this campaign will make you a target?"

"Somebody has to take a stand," David said. "I'm a Quebecer, too. And I won't become a second-class citizen just because my first language is English."

The finished story, complete with color photo, made the *Chronicle*'s front page. Turned inside and ran sixteen column inches. It began:

A Montreal bookseller is urging people who oppose Quebec's new language law to join him in a campaign of civil disobedience. David Nelligan, owner of Calypso Canada Books, is calling on merchants to post bilingual signs and go to jail if necessary.

Nelligan, a Montreal native who speaks fluent French, re-hung a bilingual sign on the front of his store yesterday: *Librairie Calypso Canada / Calypso Canada Books.* Inside the bookstore he put up a poster urging people to attend a meeting to launch the campaign, called Calypso 101....

28 / THE MAKING
OF STICK-FIGURE ANGLOS

Back at his desk in the empty house, thumbing through *Le Diable Entre Nous*, David turned up a passage poking fun at the sorcerer's parents and marvelled again at how lucky he'd been. His father read French newspapers, watched French TV, listened to French radio — yet didn't know the novel existed. Except for *Le Devoir* and a couple of obscure radio programs, the mainstream media had ignored the book.

In Isabelle's novel, the villain's parents live in a Westmount mansion. His father is a business executive who gallivants around the world in a company jet, while his mother throws tea parties and raises funds for the federal Liberals. They're stick-figure Anglos, one-dimensional blockheads — the privileged offspring of capitalist exploiters who never belonged in Quebec.

Isabelle painted a vivid scene in which her heroine, visiting Westmount for the first time, gets into an argument with the sorcerer's father over his business activities in South Africa, winds up accusing him of exploiting blacks the way his ancestors exploited French Canadians.

David had to laugh. Novelists inevitably reshape reality to suit their politics, but this approached farce. His father sprang not from the exploiting but the exploited classes. As did most remaining Anglos. And the only fitting analogy to be drawn from South Africa would focus on those who believed in the primacy of collective rights, and so identify nationalist Quebecers with pro-apartheid Afrikaners.

Isabelle's most cynical touch was that the house she described as belonging to her villain's parents was the one in which she grew up. Not in Westmount but Outremont, on the other side of the mountain. Just around the corner from Pierre Trudeau. That's where, when she wasn't away at a private school, Isabelle spent her childhood — in a three-storey brick mansion on a crescent lined with shade trees.

She'd rebelled against all that, of course. While studying at the Sorbonne, in Paris, she'd eloped with a Swiss history professor — definitely not *un de nous-autres*. With Kurt, she'd lived in Africa and Mexico and the United States. Even so, she'd retained certain attitudes about English-speaking Quebecers.

Knowing this, and knowing also that his mother wanted him to get back with Arianna, David had avoided introducing Isabelle to his parents. She kept insisting, however, and finally he broached the idea. At first his mother flatly refused. "You and Arianna were perfect together," she said. "I don't understand this separation."

"We just grew apart, Mum." He'd kept secret Isabelle's role, but knew his mother suspected interference.

"You don't walk away from a marriage at the first sign of trouble," she said. "Especially not one that was working as well as yours. You two were so good together. Maybe you should get back together and have children? At least see a marriage counsellor."

David scoffed and pleaded and eventually his mother agreed to meet Isabelle. His father was ready to go along with whatever she decided, and one Saturday afternoon David brought his "older woman" to visit.

This was October, 1975. David's parents had recently bought a modest townhouse in Verdun — a respectable, working-class neighborhood, half-English, half-French, consisting mostly of row houses and apartment blocks with metal staircases winding to the sidewalk.

David's parents welcomed Isabelle for his sake. While he hung coats and jackets in the hall, his father, speaking French, ushered her into the front room, where he'd switched off the football game.

David, his father and Isabelle sat making small talk while his mother scurried back and forth to the kitchen, declining offers of help. She was having difficulty following the conversation. As people sat down to eat at the kitchen table, and having failed with hints, David said, "Hey, everybody, let's talk English."

Isabelle slapped her forehead and addressed his mother: "David tells me your maiden name was *Granger?*" She pronounced it the French way. "And that your ancestors were among the original *Acadiens?*"

"Granger," his mother said, using the English pronounciation. "That's what the records say, yes."

"Forgive my curiosity, but David tells me you were raised English Protestant. How did that happen?"

"You hear all kinds of stories," his mother said. "One of my ancestors made the switch."

David said: "Fell in love with an Indian princess."

"My father insisted on telling crazy stories. You couldn't believe a word he said. Please, have a muffin."

His mother refused to discuss their ancestral heritage. Sitting at his desk on Old Orchard Avenue, David wondered at her prescience. But he'd already told Isabelle about his boyhood trip to Nova Scotia, and how the highlight came when his grandfather took him to see the church at Grand Pré and showed him documents pertaining to his Acadian ancestors. They were among the fourteen thousand expelled from Nova Scotia in the 1750s, ostensibly because they refused to take an oath of allegiance, really because the British wanted their land.

At the Expulsion, according to the papers his grandfather produced, his Acadian forefather, Jean-Louis Granger, had a wife, four sons, two daughters, three grandchildren, two bullocks, three cows, two horses, four sheep and six hogs. The British confiscated his farm and livestock, but Jean-Louis was one of the lucky ones — they deported him only as far as Boston.

A few years later, his grandfather said, with Nova Scotia crying for settlers, Jean-Louis and his family returned home. He exchanged an oath of allegiance for an inferior tract of land on Cobequid Bay, near the township of Hamel. But at least he was among his own people.

David had asked then how his mother had come to be raised in English, and the old man explained that the shift happened fifty years after Jean-Louis, when Télésphore Granger, his great grandson, took up with an Iroquois girl while studying for the priesthood. Discovered, and called upon to explain, the young man claimed he'd had a vision — that God had ordered him to tutor this girl.

His superiors attempted reasoning and ended up threatening excommunication. Telesphore disappeared into the night with his

Iroquois princess. Eventually, the couple produced six children: "Raised 'em as English-speaking Protestants — every last one of 'em."

David remembered his grandfather cackling into the silence of the church, claiming that he'd survived at Vimy Ridge only because he had Iroquois blood. He'd crawled through mud for hundreds of yards, he said, while directly overhead the bullets flew: "I'm part Mohawk warrior."

In Verdun, David said: "Tell Isabelle about Vimy Ridge."

But his mother refused to be drawn.

David did get her reminiscing briefly about the Second World War, when as a small-town girl, eighteen years old, she'd moved to Halifax and begun waitressing at the Air Force base. Gerard Nelligan was the best dancer she'd ever met. He waltzed her around the ballroom floor, crooning along with Frank Sinatra: *Dream, that's the thing to do/ Dream, your dreams might come true.*

Gerard bought her flowers, took her to restaurants. He told her about Montreal, about streetcars and movie theatres and visiting the Lookout on Mount Royal. And when finally he proposed, at a candle-lit dinner, she'd blushed, sipped her apple juice and said yes.

All this turned up undisguised in *Le Diable Entre Nous*, where it lent the rest credibility.

"You've lived in Montreal for how long?" Isabelle had said. "Almost thirty years? And still you don't speak French?"

"I've tried," his mother said. "I've taken courses. But with five kids to raise, and working part-time to help out, well, it just never took."

His mother's response, David noted, had failed to make the novel. Likewise what Isabelle said later, as they drove back to Outremont: "You told me your parents were poor, David, but they're English, after all. I didn't know what to expect. Then I walked into that shabby townhouse — *quelle surprise!*"

29 / REVELATIONS

Working-class Anglos? The idea flew in the face of conventional wisdom. Hence Isabelle's surprise. David found himself remembering the year in which all of Bonaventure High School had participated in a pre-Christmas competition, classroom against classroom. Every day the principal got on the intercom and urged students to bring food into school — food for the poor people. The class that brought in the most food would win the grand prize: free passes to the Saturday matinée.

Everyone wanted to win. Still, he'd been amazed at how much food some of his classmates brought: jars of pickles and olives and cranberry sauce, ten-pound bags of potatoes. Whole turkeys, two kids brought. David contributed two cans of soup his mother gave him — food for the poor people. He packed these cans into cardboard boxes at the back of the classroom.

A few days before Christmas, David was playing hockey out front of the house, firing lifters into the snowbank, when a silver station wagon pulled up beside him. Two men got out. One of them pulled a scrap of paper out of his pocket and complained to his partner that he couldn't read the address. To David he said: "This the Nelligan place?"

David said yes and fired another lifter. The men went to the back of the station wagon, grabbed two cardboard boxes and started up the driveway. The boxes were full of food. They were just like the ones he'd helped pack at school.

"Hey, you're making a mistake!" he called after the men. "That food's for the *poor* people."

The men hesitated, but his mother appeared at the top of the stairs. "What a wonderful surprise!" Red-faced and flustered, she was holding open the door. "I don't know what we would have done. Thank you. Thank you so much."

Even during the good years, David reflected now, his parents couldn't afford to keep a car on the road. His father travelled to work by taxi. A solo trip cost two dollars — awfully expensive. But at train time Old Leroux ran a flat-rate service to Bonaventure, thirty-five cents a head.

Each morning, his father would travel to the office with commuters bound for Montreal. After work, he'd walk to the Bonaventure station and ride home with the same gang. That's how David knew: whenever his father didn't arrive according to the train schedule, probably he'd gone drinking with the boys.

Usually, this meant nothing. When he got home, he'd wander around the kitchen, fix himself something to eat, then stumble off to bed. Once in a while, his mother would yell at him to stop making so much noise and they'd get into a shouting match. David would pull his pillow over his head to drown it out. After about half an hour, the fighting would stop and he'd fall back to sleep.

Then came the night his father banged into the house muttering. He slammed the door and David woke knowing something was wrong. Quarter to twelve, no trains due. Maybe his father had gone drinking with Fraticelli. Now he was pacing around the kitchen, making a slapping sound — pounding his fist into his hand?

"Fourteen years I gave them." He knocked over a kitchen chair. "Fourteen years of my life!"

"Gerard, stop slamming around out there. What are you so upset — oh my God! Look at this mess!" His mother had emerged into the kitchen. "You're like a two-year-old. Don't have enough sense to take off your boots when you come through the door."

"Don't start, Nellie." His father banged his fist on the kitchen table, rattling the utensils. "Not tonight."

"Then take your boots off!"

His father resumed pacing. "I'll take my boots off when I'm ready." He banged a cupboard door shut — once, twice.

David had never heard him this bad. His mother must have noticed because she changed her tone: "Gerard, what's happened?"

"He got me, Nellie."

"Who got you? What are you talking about?"

"That bastard at work — Grenier! Fourteen years I gave them."

"What do you mean, he got you?"

"He fired me, Nellie."

"Oh, my God."

"That big story I wrote? The Laliberté murder?"

"What about it?"

"The murderers tied up his wife, Laliberté's wife, in the next room."

"Horrible, just horrible."

"She heard the killers talking to each other in English. She couldn't be sure, but she thought they had French accents."

"So you told me."

"Yes, and that's what I wrote. But that's not what we're running. I read the proof this afternoon. The story says only that she heard the killers speaking English."

"Every story gets edited."

"Not like that, Nellie. At first I thought it was a mistake. But when I pointed it out, Grenier told me to leave it alone. He said he didn't want to upset readers with unfounded speculations. She heard the killers speaking English and that was that."

"Here, drink this." His mother had fetched a glass of water.

His father gulped it down, then continued. "I said he was rewriting the story to suit his politics, and that we should change it back. He said no way — that I was getting too big for my britches. If I didn't like the way he ran *La Victoire*, I could get the hell out. I said fine and that was that."

"He's been looking for an excuse."

"What are we going to do, Nellie? We've got bills to pay."

"Never mind, Gerry."

Was that his father sobbing?

"Never mind, now. We'll work it out."

30 / THE SECRET
OF ISABELLE'S CLAIRVOYANCE

Unusual psychic powers related to her gifts as a novelist. That was the only possible explanation. Some mild form of clairvoyance. Mental telepathy. How else to account for the way Isabelle ferreted out my every secret thought? It was spooky. So I reflected as, late one afternoon, I made for the sentry box overlooking the Mediterranean to scribble notes and dream of Arianna.

Halfway up the hill, I realized I'd forgotten my pen. Back to the flat I strode, swung up the stairs and down the hall. I opened my study door and: "What the —"

Isabelle sat at my desk, writing in her journal. There, open in front of her, lay Arianna's latest letter. The truth dawned. Isabelle had dug that letter out of my files. She'd been copying it. Now, red-faced, without a word, she jumped to her feet and, hugging her journal to her chest, dashed past me out the door.

Stunned, I sat down on my cot. After about ten minutes, I marched down the hall and tried the door to her study. Found it locked: "Isabelle, I want to talk."

I rattled the handle.

"Go away! Leave me alone."

I went for a long walk — though first I locked my study door. Not just because of the letters, but also because I feared, irrationally, that Isabelle might do something to my work-in-progress.

That evening, alone, I ate dinner at a taverna. My shock turned to anger. I couldn't believe the bad faith. When I arrived home, I found Isabelle packing. But I'd worked up a full head of steam. "I can't believe you'd stoop so low — not just to reading my private letters, but actually to copying them. You've been beavering away like that every afternoon, haven't you? Ever since the freighter."

"It's your own fault," she said. "You've driven me mad."

Isabelle started to weep. She couldn't take it any more, knowing I was going to leave. She'd started hallucinating. Probably she should visit a doctor, but he'd institutionalize her and she couldn't survive that. I had to help her leave this place. Yes, yes, she'd known from the start I'd be leaving for Africa. But she'd thought she was stronger than she was. Now she was in splinters. She no longer trusted herself. She fell to her knees. "I can't do it alone, David. You have to help me leave."

We spent the next couple of hours packing and then crashed, exhausted.

Early next morning, I helped Isabelle carry her suitcases to the bus stop. She talked, continuously, in a familar vein. Reminded me that, as a child, whenever she played musical chairs, she was always the one who ended up without a place to sit. She knew Arianna and I belonged together. "I think she's special, David — that she's very brave and centred. And her feeling for you is special, too."

It probably wouldn't have worked at Christmas, she said, the three of us here in Apolakia. But she'd left presents in her cupboard for both of us. She didn't know what she'd do now, but if she remained in Athens, she'd love to have a farewell drink with me. Also see Arianna — maybe have a drink with her, too.

The previous night, as I'd fallen asleep, I'd thought of asking Isabelle to hand over the journal into which she'd copied Arianna's letters — but the right moment never came.

Suddenly, she was gone.

I went for a long walk, then returned to the flat and wrote Arianna. I outlined what had happened — my discovery, Isabelle's departure — and confessed I'd seriously considered trying to phone Arianna, just to hear her voice. Finally had to face facts: get a phone call through from Apolakia to Wajadili? "But seventeen days, Arianna! In just seventeen days, you fly here to Greece and we begin picking up pieces. I love you, Arianna. Never stopped loving you. It'll be so good, so good just to be with you again."

I might move into my study, I said, where I felt closest to her, probably because of the maps I'd hung on the walls. Though I didn't know whether I wanted to sleep and work in the same room. Also, I wanted to retain possession of the entire floor, so we'd have it when she arrived. "I still think I should finish my rewrite here in Apolakia, where I began it. Feel I owe that to Isabelle, somehow."

Now, re-reading my letter all these years later, I'm appalled at the extent of Isabelle's influence over me. I'd discovered her treachery, recognized the profundity of her betrayal — yet still felt I owed it to her to remain in Apolakia. Also, I have to laugh at how easy I thought it would be: Isabelle had departed for Athens and that was that. Ha!

The day after she left, as if in demonstration that Isabelle did, indeed, possess certain occult powers, the winter rains hit Apolakia. Suddenly I was cooped up alone, freezing cold, in the flat we'd shared for three months. Given even a miserably overcast day, I could have gone and sat on the beach. But no. Rain and cold, rain and cold, freezing rain and cold all day, every day, non-stop.

I donned my thickest work shirt, two sweaters and a jacket — and still I froze. I couldn't hike in the hills because rain had turned them to mud. Couldn't even sit at an outdoor café and drink ouzo. Late afternoon, desperate for fresh air, I'd don my orange poncho and hike half a mile up the highway. Arrive home soaked to the skin.

To Arianna, I wrote tortured letters. And I began worrying about Isabelle. Told myself she might be better off away from me. After all, she claimed I'd driven her crazy. Trouble was: where could she go now? Back to Montreal? I imagined her weeping in some Athens hotel room. Spell it out? I doubted her stability. Knew she was depressed. Thought she might kill herself.

Then, on the same day, two letters arrived.

The first came from Athens. Isabelle had taken a room at the Hotel Cleo, just off Syntagma Square, and didn't know what she'd do next. If she had somewhere to go, she wrote, she'd be out of Athens like a shot. As it was, maybe we could all three spend Christmas in Athens and then she'd go wherever? She rambled on as only she could.

The second letter, addressed to Isabelle, came from Paris — from Chantal Leclerc, her expatriate writer-friend. I knew Isabelle had written her suggesting that, once I'd left, they tour southern France. In my reaction to these two letters, one of which I hadn't read but simply forwarded, I recognize my deepest feelings.

We're killing each other, Isabelle, can't you see that? You say you're not well. Why not? Because of me. It's me you've got to get away from. And you're not the only one who's unwell. I walk around dizzy and sick. Isabelle, we've been destroying each other. Maybe, as you suggest, it's the situation. You couldn't stand the fact of my leaving and lashed out. But what makes you think you can stand it any better now, in Athens?

Original plans? Yet another "original plan" called for Arianna and I to spend a week alone in Athens, then for the three of us to share Christmas here. You moved out, remember? So much for that "original plan." Your new scenario calls for sharing Christmas in Athens. A new beginning.

Isabelle, I'm tired of plans. The communal-house idea is dead. You decided that by leaving. This on-again, off-again scenario sounds plausible enough — for you. One year you live with your nationalist friends, the next you live with me. Isabelle, we've gone over this how many times? What about Arianna? What's she supposed to do when she's not living with me?

You've arranged your life around your literary career and your politics. That's fine. But I'm not building my life around yours. From now on,

Isabelle, I'm making my own plans. You were right to leave Apolakia. In the name of survival, you took charge of your life. Now, I'm taking charge of mine. We're down to survival, Isabelle, and I will fight to stay alive.

Who was it said that loving is letting go? Let me go, Isabelle. When you left, I realized that if you'd stayed, we would have ended up hating each other. Let me go now. By moving to Athens, you've already taken the first step. Take the second. I'm enclosing a letter from Chantal Leclerc. Go to France, Isabelle. Have a great time. Later, when we've all cooled down, we'll create a new relationship. But I can't build a life with two women at once. I've tried and failed. Time to pick up the pieces.

31 / CALYPSO REVENGE

Shortly after midnight the telephone rang and jerked David back from Greece. He expected a call, though, and gambled: "Happy anniversary!"

"Ha! Thought I'd surprise you."

"Get out of town. Or, no, let me rephrase that."

"I've been remembering the day we married."

"The bed-and-breakfast place we stayed at?"

"That impossibly soft bed? We kept rolling into the middle!"

"And next morning the landlady wouldn't shut up?"

They laughed at the shared memories.

Then: "Arianna, I wish you were home here. You and the kids."

"I wish we were, too."

Into the silence, David said, "How are the kids, anyway?"

"They're fine. They miss their Dad. They've just gone down. Stayed up late to watch a movie."

"So here we sit on our annivarsary, a thousand miles apart. It's ridiculous."

"But we're still together, David. That's what I wanted to say. I didn't mean it earlier, about not coming back to Montreal."

"I know that."

"I get tired of the politics, the constant struggle. But I know how you feel about Montreal. And you're right. We can rebuild the bookstore. David?"

For an instant, he'd gone silent. But no, he couldn't bring himself to talk about Isabelle's latest gambit. Not yet. Instead, he said, "Yesterday I visited the store, did I tell you? Started cleaning up the mess."

"How's it look?"

A few moments later, having air-brushed the truth about the bookstore and said goodbye with tears in his voice, David found himself remembering that night just three weeks before, when for the second time in five minutes, as he lolled on the floor playing Triple Yahtzee with the kids, the telephone rang.

On the tape deck, Lord Executor had been disparaging the Great Houdini and, not incidentally, launching a full-scale Calypso War: *At last the hour of vengeance is at hand: / I am in the land.*

After three rings, as another Calypsonian, Lord Caresser, took charge of the assault, the ringing stopped.

Remembering, now, David picked up his rediscovered bongos and began tapping away, absentmindedly. *Those who boast Houdini can sing, / In my opinion they know nothing. / For it's all propaganda, deceit and pretense, / he hasn't got the shadow of intelligence.*

Again the phone began to ring. That was the signal: three rings, stop and start. David nodded permission and Emile picked up the receiver. The boy's eyes went wide: "Daddy, it's Uncle T."

David took the phone. "Tolbert, what's up?"

"The bookstore's on fire!"

"The bookstore? Tolbert, if this is —"

"No joke, David. Just got a call from the janitor across the street. Says he heard this noise, like a small explosion. Looks out his window and the bookstore's glowing red. He tried phoning you but got no answer."

The fire department was on the way.

As David banged down the receiver, Time went strange. He raced to the hall cupboard, felt like he was running underwater. Yet the music played on. Roaring Lion joined the Calypso onslaught: *Destruction, desolation and damnation, / All these I'll inflict on insubordination.*

Moving in slow motion, David grabbed his ski jacket. The kids sat watching, wide-eyed. He'd leave them with the woman next door. No, wait. Tonight she played bridge. Snapping back into real time, David cried: "Get your coats! The bookstore's on fire!"

David led the kids out the back door and into the garage. Loaded them into his beater and sped east along Sherbrooke, with Lord Executor and Roaring Lion still fighting a Calypso War in his head: *At last the hour of vengeance is at hand: / I am in the land.*

Snowplows had cleared the road. Traffic was light. At red lights, David didn't stop, just slowed down and honked. He managed the half-hour drive in twelve minutes. Found fifty or sixty people milling around out front of the bookstore. They stomped their feet and flapped their arms against the cold. Two firetrucks sat in the street, red lights flashing in circles. Half a dozen firefighters paraded around in yellow raincoats and black hip-waders, waving their arms, telling people to move back. Others were putting away hoses.

David pulled up onto the sidewalk, told the kids to stay in the car. He jumped out and pushed through the crowd. A firefighter tried to stop him. David hollered, "I own the store!"

The man let him pass.

The front door hung loose off its hinges. The bookstore stank of fire and water and something else. Gasoline? Fire had roared through the front room, reducing his stock to tissue paper. A few dozen hardcovers lay in soggy piles on the floor. The shelving was beyond salvage. Weak in the knees, David kept moving. *At last the hour of vengeance is at hand: / I am in the land.*

Fire had gutted the back room, too. The damage was worse than in front. He stumbled over to his desk, found it piled high with charred rubble. Same with the chair behind it, no place to sit down. Leaning against the desk, David noticed that a side window had been smashed. He stepped towards it, kicked something. Looked down and saw the pipe. Three inches across, maybe two feet long, stoppered at both ends.

He waved a fireman over, pointed.

"Tabernaque!" the man cried. *"Une hostie de bombe!"*

Firefighters scrambled out of the store with David on their heels. The crowd had grown. Emmanuel Tolbert was there, behind a yellow cord, arguing with a fireman. He stopped talking when David arrived. Wordlessly, the two men hugged. Emile and Suzanne jumped out of the car and ran to him, and David let them stay, each of them holding a hand.

After a while, the bomb sqaud arrived — three men wearing masks and padded suits — and carried sandbags into the bookstore.

"Daddy, what are they doing?"

"I don't know."

"They pack those bags around the pipebomb," Tolbert said. "Then they detonate it. Ka-boom!"

Twenty minutes later, when it came, the explosion rattled windows in the apartment buildings around them. Strange thing was, instead of echoing away to nothing, the blast gathered force. Shock waves reverberated among the downtown highrises, then thundered off the island of Montreal and rolled out across Quebec, shaking buildings and levelling houses before sweeping across the rest of the country, so that Canadians from coast to coast tore their hair and cried: "Earthquake! The hour of vengeance! Must be the end of the world!"

32 / WOMAN'S HEAD AND PORTRAIT

"Daddy, what if you'd been working late?"

Outside the bookstore, the explosion reverberating around them, David had patted his son's arm. But three weeks later, alone in the house on Old Orchard Avenue, remembering, he said aloud: "Never mind, Emile. No way they're driving me out of Montreal."

David spoke to hear the sound of a voice, any voice, even his own, as he knelt at the fireplace striking match after match. And realized, hearing himself, that he was more firmly resolved than ever. With the bilingual sign, in the early days, he'd let vandals intimidate him. Instead of taking a stand, as Tolbert had urged, he'd looked for an easy way out. For a Canadian compromise. And found it.

Story of my life, he thought, disgusted.

The paper caught, finally, and David sat back on his heels and watched as fire ignited the kindling. Remembered the autumn of 1975, when the easy way out had been to move into the Outremont house.

Isabelle had been right about space: they had oodles. They talked about having separate bedrooms, but not seriously. Agreed to share the big one she'd slept in alone. More intensely, they debated who would occupy which study. The main-floor study, next to the kitchen, was cosy but subject to interruptions. David pointed out that most of these involved Isabelle's nationalist friends, and finally she let him have the study out back — though later, in *Le Diable Entre Nous*, she told the world how deeply she resented this.

Household chores presented no real problems. They divided the cooking duties — though Isabelle outshone him in the kitchen — and designated Sunday pot-luck. Saturday was cleaning day. They split the house into areas and rotated, tackled two out of three each week: living room and dining room, bathrooms and halls, kitchen by itself. David was stunned at how much extra work it took to run a house — carry out the garbage, trim the hedge, fix the hinge on the back door.

Still, they achieved a routine. David would rise at five in the morning, head out back into his heated study and work on the novel that would serve as his master's thesis. At eight he'd come back inside and eat breakfast with Isabelle. Often, they'd sit drinking coffee and she'd ramble on about her ex-husband and what a scumbag he'd been — sorting it out for her next novel.

As September became October and then November, David began to tire of Isabelle's relentless self-obsession. He recalled a painting he'd seen in Paris, a Picasso called Woman's Head and Portrait. On an otherwise serene self-portrait, the artist had superimposed the head of a howling woman. Now, as day after day he endured Isabelle's monologues, that painting gained resonance.

Still, by ten o'clock, David would be back at his typewriter. He'd write until one, then eat lunch and go about his business. His grad-student fellowship meant he had to teach a section of first-year English, and three afternoons a week he'd ramble around a classroom waving his arms, trying to interest would-be engineers in Yeats or Whitman or D.H. Lawrence. Evenings, he'd read, plan classes, mark essays — and go for long walks.

Meanwhile, to bring in money, Isabelle ran writing workshops, two of them at the house. Students would turn up unannounced, adding to the cacaphony of her political circle. Usually, David just opened the door. He'd become invisible. When he did register, it wasn't as himself, but as the famous writer's Anglais — her English play-thing. He saw little of Emmanuel Tolbert, who was busy earning bylines at *The Montreal Standard*, and lots of Philippe Lachapelle, the most tolerant of Isabelle's nationalist friends, probably because he was gay.

Arianna quickly became an issue, but here David dug in his heels. That, at least, he had to grant himself. Once a week he'd meet her to exchange the Volkswagen. They'd go for a coffee or a milk shake, or up onto Mount Royal just to walk around, kicking at autumn leaves. Every time he saw her, David remarked how attractive she was, so tall and trim and athletic, so exotic-looking, with her thick red hair and big brown eyes.

On returning from Timmins, she'd taken a flat on Durocher, just around the corner from the "dinky little apartment" they'd shared on Aylmer. Arianna was completing a degree in architecture and design, but with a minor in art, and lately she'd been painting —

huge, angry canvasses at first, but then a series built around the idea of rebirth. Three of these she'd sold.

When they met to exchange the Volkswagen, Arianna might mention a movie she'd seen, a restaurant she'd visited — even, obliquely, another man she'd dated. Several times she raised the subject of divorce. David would say: "What's the rush?"

"I want to get on with my life."

"Looks to me like you're doing just fine."

"What's that supposed to mean?"

"Please, Arianna. I don't think I can handle it."

"Maybe you should have thought of that."

David would say nothing. In the end, shaking her head, Arianna would let the subject drop. And only once did she bring up Isabelle. They'd climbed the wooden stairs to The Lookout and stood leaning against the balustrade, staring out at the Montreal skyline. Arianna had met a female friend of Kurt's at a vernissage in Old Montreal, an older woman: "She said she felt sorry for you. That you didn't know what you'd got yourself into. 'Isabelle's going to wring him out like a sponge,' she said. 'Squeeze him dry and throw him away.'"

"That's Kurt talking. Nobody's going to wring me out. I'm just as talented as Isabelle — maybe more."

"You're also fourteen years younger."

33 / ESCALATING UNPLEASANTNESS

Why did David need to visit with Arianna every time they exchanged the Volkswagen? That's what Isabelle wanted to know. She felt the same way about his estranged wife as he did about her ex-boyfriend, Jacques Bienvenue. And for David's sake she'd stopped seeing Jacques by himself, and got together with him only as part of a circle.

This David called a false parallel. Isabelle's life teemed with people, he said — writer friends, political friends. And every other weekend she had her sons. True, she was older, and she'd developed these relationships over the years. Fact remained, his own situation differed radically. For five years, Arianna had been everything to him: wife, lover, friend. He'd sacrificed the Jacques-Bienvenue aspect of his life with Arianna, the sexual side, he said. But the rest he refused to give up.

"The trouble with you, David, is that you want both of us."

"Wasn't it you, Isabelle, who railed against 'the couply stuff' Lawrence detested? Argued that Sartre and de Beauvoir found a way beyond it?"

Round they went. They'd said it all before. But Isabelle wouldn't leave it alone. Usually, they argued in French. But one night, soon after he arrived home, she greeted him with a blast of English: "You screwed her tonight, didn't you?"

Astonished, David burst out laughing: "What?"

"You damn blockhead! I can smell it on you. You were out screwing your wife while I was at home here, washing your dirty underwear."

She'd been doing no such thing. Nor had David been sleeping with Arianna. When he suggested that probably Isabelle smelled gasoline because he'd filled up the Volks, she called him a barefaced liar. He replied, still laughing, that she could believe whatever she wished. And walked away.

During yet another attack, in the kitchen after breakfast one morning, David was leaning back in his chair with his arms folded across his chest. Isabelle threw her coffee at him. He ducked and tumbled backwards, onto the floor. Sprained his wrist badly enough that he couldn't type for two days.

The question is: Why didn't he leave?

Faced with such escalating unpleasantness, why didn't he pack his bags and clear out? Say *au revoir* and rent an apartment or, temporarily, a room. They weren't hard to find. More than a dozen years later, rambling around the empty house on Old Orchard, refusing to acknowledge his growing tiredness, David could produce no easy answer.

First try: People were like planets. Fourteen years older, centuries wiser, Isabelle had pulled him out of his own orbit and into hers. Second try: archetypal experience. He'd fallen under the spell of some primeval complex, locked onto some fixed pattern of behaviour, and like it or not, his course was fixed. Third try: he'd become a character in one of Isabelle's novels. He enjoyed the illusion of free will. But in truth he was trapped until she decided to release him.

Turning to specifics, David found none that reflected well on his younger self. He'd grown comfortable, for example. For the first time in his life, he had a private space in which to work — the study out back — and he didn't want to relinquish that.

Less damagingly, perhaps: he'd bought into the idea that Isabelle was good for him as a writer. He enjoyed her wit, her broad education. Intellectually, she challenged him, made him look at himself. Finally: when he'd moved into the house, early in September, he'd promised to remain until Christmas. An observer might find here a smidgen of baffled honor — but David knew the truth. He'd seen what Isabelle had done, in her fiction, to people who broke promises.

Even so, to remain through that endless autumn, he needed help — insulation. And he found it in dry red wine. Two or three nights a week, while Isabelle talked politics with her circle, David would knock back a couple of glasses, then pull on his duffle coat and scarf, his Russian-looking hat with ear flaps, and plunge into the night to ramble the icy, tree-lined streets of Outremont.

Early on, he'd contemplate his novel-in-progress. He was replaying the psychedelic sixties — orgies and acid trips — against childhood scenes of growing up in a French-Catholic town. Phrases and images would come to him as he walked. He carried a notebook and he'd whip off his right glove and stand scribbling under streetlamps.

He wouldn't allow himself to think of Arianna until late in the walk. Then he'd spot a back alley or an empty park — somewhere nobody would see him. Arianna! Where are you tonight? More than once, in a deserted school yard he'd discovered, David leaned against a wall and wept.

One night, after crying himself out against that wall, David hit upon the idea of taking a short trip. Get away and think, maybe visit Quebec City. For the fictional hero of his work-in-progress, one Frankie McCracken, he needed ancestors. That was it. He'd take the bus to Quebec City and plunder the archives.

Over coffee next morning, he broached the idea gingerly. Noted that, during the past three months, Isabelle had twice got out of Montreal — once to attend a meeting of the *Union des écrivains,* another time to sit on a Canada Council jury. Meanwhile, he'd gone nowhere.

Isabelle didn't blink. She knew David wanted to stand back, get a fix on his situation. Find a way to sneak back to Arianna. In *Le Diable Entre Nous,* she admits as much. But also she knew how to respond. And this response, he realized now, she'd omitted from her novel. There, she ridiculed his possessiveness, all right. But nowhere did she even hint that she knew precisely how to exploit it.

Go to Quebec City, she said. Have a good time. "Don't worry," she added, apropos of nothing: "I won't go out with Jacques Bienvenue while you're away."

David looked at her with surprise: "It never occurred to me that you would."

34 / PRESS CONFERENCE

The Saturday morning after the firebombing, David talked with police. He told them what time, exactly, he'd left the bookstore (ten past six), whether he'd noticed any strangers lurking (no), or anything else unusual (no). Then nothing. He called the police Sunday and again Monday morning. Yes, they said, it looked like arson. But they hadn't yet begun investigating. They were short-staffed. He'd have to wait his turn.

What? Too short-staffed to investigate a case of politically moti-vated arson? Outraged, David responded like the ex-journalist he was, the activist he was becoming. He telephoned every newspaper and television station in the city. Invited them to attend a Wednes-day morning press conference at the burned-out bookstore.

The turnout exceeded his expectations — half a dozen newspa-per reporters, three TV crews, assorted friends and strangers. David stood under bright lights while cameras whirred and read, in French and English both, what he considered a measured statement.

"Early this morning," he read, starting in French, "the Montreal police confirmed in a radio broadcast what everybody already knew. The fire that ravaged this bookstore, Calypso Canada Books, was the result of arson. Some unknown person or persons broke into the store, doused the back room with gasoline and tossed a Molotov cocktail through the window before escaping."

"*C'est confirmé?*" A woman's voice.

"As of this morning, yes. Many of you already know that. What most people don't know, however," David resumed reading, "but the Montreal police do know, is that for the past few weeks people have been phoning the bookstore with threats. Warning part-time workers, most of them students, to find other jobs."

The place went silent.

"What most people don't know," David continued, "but the Montreal police do know, is that vandals have repeatedly targetted this bookstore. They've painted slogans, smashed windows, dumped garbage on the front steps." He took a sip of water. "We've had threats of violence, acts of vandalism — and now we have a firebombing. All of them aimed at Quebec citizens whose only crime has been to work for an employer standing up for the rights of a minority: English-speaking Quebecers."

"Même s'ils n'en voulaient pas," came a man's voice from the back of the store. "Even if they don't want you to."

David kept reading: "Most Quebecers will condemn the fire-bombing, I know. The vast majority will dismiss it as an isolated incident, the shameful act of a few extremists. What we have to recognize, however, is that the rhetoric of these past weeks — in the media, in the Quebec national assembly, in the streets of Montreal — that rhetoric has created an atmosphere. An atmosphere that fosters criminal acts like this one."

"Rien n'est encore prouvé!"

"Surely the atmosphere of any society is the responsibility of those who live in it," David read. "I'd like to ask my fellow Quebecers: What kind of society do you want? Do you want politicians and influential journalists flinging epithets like 'white Rhodesians' at those who defend their principals? Do you want an intellectual elite that watches in silence while young people find role models in the likes of Paul Rose?"

"Paul Rose, y'a raison!"

A woman told the heckler to shut up or get out.

"What, in the end, is a democratic society? Surely it's one in which rights and freedoms apply equally to all? One in which a citizen can express a minority opinion without fear of firebombs? I remain convinced that Anglophones —"

"The Anglophones of Quebec are the best-treated minority in the world."

Tempted to abandon his text, David noticed Arianna shaking her head and resumed reading. "Anglophones have a place in Quebec. We've earned that place and need not apologize for being ourselves. I believe that Francophones and Anglophones can live and work together in harmony and mutual respect and comprehension. I also remain convinced that the latest language law is unjust and discrimi-natory, and that it abrogates a basic democratic right — the right to freedom of expression. I remain convinced that the only logical response to this unjust law is peaceful civil disobedience."

"Le Quebec aux Québécois!"

"I will not be intimidated. I will not give up my right to freedom of expression. And I will not leave this province." He'd finished the French text. Before beginning again, in English, David said: "There's more than one way to be a Quebecer."

35 / THE BROKEN NOSE

More than one way to be a Quebecer? Sometimes he wondered. David Nelligan tossed a log on the fire and knelt, staring into the flames. He found himself remembering his early days with Tolbert, roaring around the North Shore in a battered sports car. Tolbert had helped his older brother out of a jam, lying spontaneously to a cuckolded husband who'd turned up at his front door: "Yes, of course I'm sure. My brother was here with me all afternoon."

In thanks, his brother given Tolbert free use of his number-two car, an old TR3. It burned oil and overheated regularly, but the boys thought it fabulous and went joy-riding whenever they could afford gas. One Friday night, David remembered, tooling along the highway on the outskirts of Rosemere, top down, radio blaring, they spotted action at a community hall: half a dozen cars, a few teenagers standing around out front. What the hell?

Turned out to be a small dance, just a juke box and maybe a hundred kids. But a dance was a dance, the music was loud and they weren't going anyplace special. They paid their money, got their hands stamped and made their way into the darkened hall.

David realized they were the only ones in the place speaking English. Usually that was okay, though with Tolbert he worried. His friend didn't swagger, exactly. But he did walk tall. And his very existence was sometimes read as a challenge. Not only was he black, but lately he'd begun working with weights and it showed. Worst of all, he spoke no French.

All this David forgot when he recognized three girls from the summer before in Ste-Thérèse. At the *Salle de danse*, he'd worshipped from afar. Now, with Twist and Shout booming through loudspeakers, he wandered over to the prettiest of the three — a petite blonde — and led her onto the floor. They danced two or three fast ones — *Do You Love Me, The Wah-Watusi* — and when a slow song came on, *You'll Lose A Good Thing*, the girl came into his arms. He was wracking his brain for something clever to say when CRACK!

David looked over his shoulder and there was Tolbert, spread-eagled against a dozen sheets of drywall that were leaning against an old piano. The biggest guy in the place, a muscular six-footer they'd noticed at the entrance, sleeves rolled up to his shoulders, stood facing Tolbert, his arms extended.

As David watched, Tolbert come off the drywall with a fist that started at his shoulder. Smashed the big guy in the face. Down he went, blood spurting from his nose. Girls screamed. Another guy moved towards Tolbert. Without thinking, David charged across the floor and leapt onto the second guy's back. This fellow was no pipsqueak, either, and he used David's momentum to fling him over his head and onto the floor. Then kicked him in the stomach.

David took a second kick in the stomach and a third in the ribs. Six or seven guys started kicking at him. He covered his head with his hands. After a while, the kicking stopped.

David struggled to his feet beside Tolbert, found twelve or fifteen guys encircling them. The big guy who'd started the fight, obviously king of the dance hall, knelt in a corner with his face in his hands, blood gushing through his fingers.

The two English-speakers started backing towards the door. Halfway there, David remembered his jacket — a red-and-black hunting jacket he'd bought with his paper-route money. *"Mon veston."* He pointed. *"Y'est juste là. Le rouge-et-noir."*

One guy took a swing at him. *"Laisse-le, mon hostie."*

"Sois sérieux. Give me my jacket."

"Tu l'as plus, ton veston! You want to try and get it?"

David and Tolbert backed out the door and down the stairs. Still accompanied by a crowd, they crossed the parking lot. They hopped over the doors into the sports car with half a dozen guys slapping and punching at them. A cry went up from the rear of the crowd. As Tolbert started the car, a pathway opened and the big guy with the broken nose rushed up, still gushing blood. He grabbed Tolbert around the neck and began smashing at his face, trying to haul him over the side of the car.

"C'est fini!" David grabbed Tolbert's shoulder and hung on. *"C'est fini, tabernaque!"*

Tolbert had one hand on the wheel and was trying with the other to defend his face: "Put it in first!"

David jammed the gearshift forward. Tolbert lifted his foot off the clutch, cried: "The gas! Hit the gas!" David jammed his foot on the pedal. The big guy lost his grip on Tolbert and the boys fish-tailed out of the parking lot with stones whizzing around their heads.

They drove fast until they were sure nobody was following, then pulled over to let the sports car cool down. Checked each other for damage. Discovered blood on their shirts. As well, David had nail marks on his neck. His ribs ached and the left side of his forehead was scraped raw. But Tolbert had the real trophies — a gash over his right eye — already puffy, soon to turn blacker than black — and a badly cut lower lip.

Both boys were ready to call it a night, but decided to clean up before heading home. A few minutes later, in Bonaventure, Tolbert pulled into Big Joe's Restaurant, where seven or eight older guys, English-speakers, were shooting pool. Noticing the condition of the new arrivals, they asked what had happened.

The boys told them.

"Let's go clean the place out."

"How many Frenchies did you say?"

"Fuckin' Frogs!"

"Pea-soupers!"

"It's not because they're French," David said. "Tolbert broke the guy's nose."

"Christ, Nelligan. Are you English or what?"

David had said nothing about losing his jacket. But now Tolbert mentioned it and that was all the excuse anybody needed. Ten guys piled into three different cars.

"You coming, Nelligan?"

What could he do? David hopped into the TR3 and, with Tolbert, led the caravan back to Rosemere. He feared the night was going to end badly and saw with relief that the community hall was pitch black — deserted. David jumped out and looked around, but nobody had thought to leave his jacket. A couple of the guys lamented that they weren't going to break any heads. Then somebody said he knew where there was a party. The boys piled back into their cars and roared around the parking lot a few times, stirring up dust.

Later, at the party, Tolbert's scrapes and bruises made him the guest of honor. He'd broken a guy's nose. David could have shared the glory, but instead he sat in a corner eating peanuts and wondering why he felt so low.

36 / QUEBEC CITY DEBACLE

In 1975, before he left for Quebec City, David asked Tolbert to meet him at the Rymark. He needed to talk politics with an Anglophone, if only because Isabelle kept insisting that, next election, the nationalist Parti Québécois would do far better than anybody expected. Usually prescient, Tolbert scoffed and dimissed this as wishful thinking. He preferred to discuss David's private life. Quebec City was a great idea, he said. He'd run into Arianna the other day and they'd agreed: David looked like he could use a holiday.

"So now you're discussing me with Arianna."

Tolbert threw his palms in the air. He polished off a glass of draft and, then, while waving four fingers in the air, trying to catch a waiter's eye, said: "David, I hope you know what you're doing."

"Not to worry, mon." Always his West Indian accent made Tolbert laugh. "Ain't no time bombs in my future."

On Old Orchard Avenue, remembering, David winced. About his private life, at least, Tolbert had been right. This he admitted now, ruefully, looking around the living room at the explosion of books and papers. If somewhere truth existed, his only hope was to dig it out from beneath the rubble.

His trip to Quebec City had produced two documents. The first was a postcard of a winter scene, a winding street in the Old Town. "Dear Arianna," he'd written. "This while looking out at the Plains of Abraham. Six-foot snowbanks line the back streets. Here I find the same wintry peace we knew in the Rockies. Yesterday, as I rode into town on the bus, I remembered stopping in Banff the first time we travelled out West. That feeling of, hey! Look at this! Why go any further? Remember the deer? So far, though I've rambled the streets, I've found none leaping fences."

The second document was an angry letter he wrote twelve hours later — not to Arianna but Isabelle. Reading it in west-end Montreal, David shook his head disgustedly to see what a child he'd been. And how easily Isabelle had exploited that childishness.

In the end, he hadn't sent the letter. Unable to contain himself, he'd called Isabelle from a phone booth — third time that night — and read it to her long distance. Outraged, huffing and puffing. Even though earlier, he'd been thinking lonely thoughts not of Isabelle, as he claimed, but Arianna.

Funny that the most significant event of my trip to Quebec City should occur, not here in the Old Town, but back home in Montreal. Having announced that you wouldn't go out with Jacques Bienvenue while I was away, you went out with him. The rest is detail.

Obviously, if you considered my feelings at all, you dismissed them as unimportant. A political act, this. An act of aggression, a gesture which, like a slap in the face, one would like to ignore, but can't.

"What'd you do tonight?"

"Oh, I went to the movies, the Élysée, and saw a strange film starring Carole Laure and Lewis Furey. Wildly sexy but with this quirky supernatural element...."

To call you merely a liar would be to denigrate your talent. You equivocate, Isabelle. You omit, you elide, you run sentences together to preclude questions. You're not lying, exactly. But you're not telling the truth, either. How reminiscent this is of your sordid little affair with T.J.

You knew I would telephone Saturday night. I called first at quarter to twelve (a fact you disputed, in our first conversation, already preparing your defence). No answer. The movie would have ended before eleven. So, you were in no hurry to hear my voice.

Isn't it strange that, when I mentioned this trip, you thought immediately of Jacques Bienvenue? "You don't have to worry," you said, apropos of nothing, "I won't go out with Jacques while you're away."

I wonder why you changed your mind. Or if you changed your mind at all. Maybe you saw your chance: you knew from the beginning that, should Bienvenue ask you out — and you would make damn sure he knew I was away — you would go out with him. And so, from the first, you lied — lied so I would go away. Certainly, I had a sense at times that you wanted me out of town. See how well I trust you?

"We didn't go out to dinner. We didn't go out drinking."

What? Didn't he ask you? In any case, that's beside the point. You said you wouldn't go out with Jacques and you went. Period. Do I over-react? I think not. Some moments contain more than others. Joycean epiphanies, remember?

But let's be generous: a last-minute phone call, a spur-of-the-moment decision, a long movie. In itself, a small moment. But no smaller, surely, than many another epiphany. I wonder if your little outing with Jacques Bienvenue will eventually prove pivotal to a book about us?

You knew you'd be huring me. Hence your prepared defence. "So I went to the movies with Jacques Bienvenue. What's wrong with that?"

Answer: You said you wouldn't go. And then you went.

Cut to Quebec City. Quarter to one in the morning. Drunk and full of love, I trudge to the nearest phone booth: Isabelle, I've visited the archives and learned all about my great great grandfather! His birthdate, his address. Isabelle, Isabelle, earlier tonight, sitting in my hotel room sipping dry red wine, I started crying just thinking of you.

Meanwhile, you've been lying in bed, fantasizing about Jacques "let's-do-it-for-old-times-stake" Bienvenue. Or worse.

Why did you do it, Isabelle? Jealousy? Fear? A combination of the two? "Go off alone, will he? Show some independence? I'll teach him!"

But maybe I flatter myself that I was ever so much on your mind. Aware that offence is the best defence, and as if I'm at fault, you say: "There, you've got your tight voice on again."

Do you remember, Isabelle, that time you were leaving for Ottawa, early on, and I said I'd be visiting Tolbert at his farmhouse? You asked if I were bringing Arianna and said you wouldn't like it if I did. I said I wouldn't do that. And didn't.

I wonder how you would have felt, though, if when you called me from Ottawa, I told you I'd changed my mind. That I'd brought Arianna after all: "So? What's wrong with that?"

In fact, Isabelle, I know how you would have felt. Shocked. Angry. And a little sick inside.

On Old Orchard Avenue, David jumped to his feet and began storming around the living room. "You fool!" he shouted at his younger self. "She played you like a violin!"

On his return from Quebec City, Isabelle met him at the bus depot. He was still upset — so predictable — but she insisted that they sit together in a coffee shop. Hadn't he told her that he'd always wanted to visit Greece? Look! She produced travel brochures. And hadn't he always wanted to sail on a freighter? Isabelle brought forth pamphlets complete with floor plans and rates.

By next summer, she reminded him, he'd have completed his master's degree. Why not take a break? They could spend six or eight months on a Greek island, writing novels, exploring. Maybe live in a villa that looked out over the sea.

David waved his hand as if to catch her attention: "Money?"

"No problem," Isabelle said. "I'll lend you the freighter fare and we'll save the rest."

"Are you sure we can swing this?"

"*Absolument.* But we'll have to act quickly. To book a cabin, look — we'll have to mail a down payment right away. What do you say, David? Let's sail away to Greece."

37 / THE WAR MOVES TO ATHENS

In Athens, Isabelle stayed for a few days in a hotel off Syntagma Square, then rented a room in a boarding house on the outskirts of Plaka, a warren of winding streets, curiosity shops and "genuine" tavernas. Her room, she wrote in a letter, was one of three on the ground floor. She shared a bathroom and had access to the communal kitchen upstairs, where the owners lived.

Her writer-friend in Paris, she said, Chantal Leclerc, had become an acquaintance. She wasn't going to France for Christmas. I'd been cruel even to suggest it. I'd dismissed her. She insisted that I call her at the boarding house and specified a time. On the telephone, she wept and accused me of inhuman cruelty. I backed down. Yes, yes, I said. If Arianna agreed, we'd all three get together over Christmas.

To Arianna, in a much darker mood than before, I wrote outlining this latest development. Explained that Isabelle still wanted the three of us to spend Christmas together....

> To tell the truth, I'm worried about her. She's not all that stable. She talks of demons, of other selves. She can get pretty weird. Remember when you said I propped her up? I didn't see it then but I do now — that doctor-patient aspect of our relationship.
>
> At the same time, Isabelle has taught me a lot, both as a writer and about facing myself. I can't just dismiss her; and I can't speak for you. Jaysus! I guess Isabelle has made more than a scene, hasn't she? I hope you'll be kind to her, Arianna. She speaks of your courage, your integrity, your centredness.
>
> I remember telling Tolbert that I was a balloon and you held the string. Believe it or not, I'm the one who's been holding Isabelle's string. Guess you saw that before I did....

Painful reading, this. In subsequent letters, repeatedly, I insisted that Isabelle was a good person. That she had a bitter, angry side, but could also be gentle and caring. I couldn't be so cruel as to tell her no, I wouldn't see her in Athens. I couldn't say get lost, get out of my life, I don't care what happens to you. Isabelle had to understand that I was leaving. But I wanted to leave with her blessing, if I could — not her curse.

I'd understand if Arianna were angry, because part of me was angry, too. Isabelle was refusing to let me go. Not out of bloody-mindedness, necessarily. Maybe she did love me and couldn't help herself. Anyway, she'd commandeered Athens.

I've been looking at my photos of you, Arianna. Soon we'll be together again. A bit of a mess to untangle, but we can manage that, can't we? I'll be waiting for you at the airport, my love. I've got tears in my eyes, Arianna, just thinking about seeing you. I'm so sorry about everything. Oh, Love. Here you were coming to Greece and we were going to have such a good time.

But you knew all along that I'd need your help. And so I do. Just think how soon we'll be together, Arianna. I'll be at the airport. I know this is silly, this closing. All I'm trying to say is that I love you and need you. Come to me, Love. Come.

A few days later, lugging Isabelle's trunk, I travelled to Athens and made my way to the rooming house on Poukakos Street. As we sat in her rented room sipping ouzo, Isabelle showed me a letter she'd received from Philippe Lachapelle, her professor friend — the only member of her circle who'd ever been civil to me. "If you're paying the rent," he'd written of the flat in Apolakia, "the first thing to do is get Nelligan the hell out of there."

He was responding, I knew, to some howl of misery. Still, I didn't like his tone, much less his conception of me. True, I still owed Isabelle freighter fare (paid back long since). But all other expenses we'd split down the middle. Same with my thousand dollars in poker winnings. In Apolakia, she'd paid a shade more than half the rent — but she'd also taken the best room for her study.

Angered by Lachapelle's letter — what? he perceived me as a rider of coat-tails? — I plunged right back into the morass: "You told this turkey I was living off you?"

"He jumped to conclusions," Isabelle said. "I wrote him when I was upset because originally Athens was going to be our treat together, yours and mine."

"Right. But you gave up that treat so I'd remain longer in Greece. Only then you changed your mind and decided you wouldn't give it up, after all. Now you want the three of us to work out some arrangement."

"You wanted that last year, David. You talked about it often enough, how you loved two women and why couldn't we work something out? You can't just change your mind."

"I was also on my knees last year, remember? Begging you to let me go? You insisted that I keep my promise, that I take this trip to Greece."

"It's been good, hasn't it?"

"It's had its moments. But I've kept my promise. You took charge of your life when you moved to Athens. Now I'm taking charge of mine."

"You've already agreed we can see each other over Christmas, David. All three of us. Who knows? Arianna might reduce the pressure. Alone, we're too intense. But maybe we'll develop a whole new arrangement, a three-way marriage. Mutual support cutting three ways instead of two."

"Are you kidding, Isabelle? Arianna will never go for that."

"You've never witnessed a birth, David. It's painful and difficult and you think it's never going to end — but the results are worth it."

"Arianna's not going to build her life around yours, Isabelle. And neither am I."

"Let's see what she says, David. If she says yes, you have no choice but to try."

The Chronicle played David's post-firebombing press conference on the front page, straight news. And on the editorial page, it disputed his contention that civil disobedience was the only sane response to Quebec's absurd language laws.

This he'd expected.

But the reaction of the French press shocked him. Mainstream editorials accused him of grandstanding, railed against his "truculent posturing," claimed he was denigrating the province's Francophone majority. And the tabloids went further, especially *La Nouvelle de Montréal*.

In west-end Montreal, alone in the night and slapping away on his bongo drums, too wired to sleep, David wondered: Was he going to sacrifice his life to this cause? Maybe his arrogance was once again getting the best of his common sense? What was he trying to prove?

After reading his public statement in the bombed-out bookstore, David had responded to questions. A reporter in wire-rimmed glasses had asked innocently what he thought of the police investigation. He played right into the guy's hands, he saw now, demanding to know why the police hadn't acted immediately to find the culprits. Why were they dragging their feet? To him the answer was obvious. Somebody had set the fire in response to his civil-liberties campaign. And the police didn't want to know.

Before writing, the Nouvelle reporter had taken his comments to the police and invited reaction. An anonymous spokesman, obviously stung, responded by declaring that the police had not eliminated David himself as an arson suspect. Perhaps he'd set fire to his own bookstore to gain publicity for Calypso 101?

This was the angle *La Nouvelle* sought. Under a headline, "All roads lead to Nelligan," and quoting unidentified sources, the tabloid spun out a story asserting that David Nelligan himself was the prime suspect in the arson investigation.

Ever since launching Calypso 101, David had been under attack in the French media. But this arson allegation went beyond vicious. This was libel. After conferring with Tolbert and a lawyer-acquaintance, David filed notice of a million-dollar libel suit against *La Nouvelle de Montréal*: $750,000 for damages to his reputation and $250,000 in punitive damages.

This produced more headlines. More telephone threats. One caller mentioned the Nelligan children and where they attended school. Next afternoon, Emile arrived home from a classmate's birthday party with a black eye. Kids had taunted him about his father, the firebomber. "Dad, you didn't start that fire, did you?"

Next day a suburban mayor, well-known for his nationalist sympathies, suggested on TV that David had insulted the Québécois nation. He, for one, felt traumatized. The mayor didn't know whether this Nelligan was guilty of arson or not. The law stipulated a presumption of innocence. But if, one day, the police found evidence that this man had set fire to his own bookstore simply to discredit the Québécois nation, obviously the province would have no choice but to declare independence.

Say what?

The following afternoon, having picked up his daughter from figure-skating class, David arrived home to find a dozen reporters parked outside the house. Someone had tipped them that the police were coming to arrest him for arson. This was turning into a Kafka novel. David rushed into the house and found Arianna in tears: "Oh, God, David! I've been so worried."

Little Suzanne started to cry: "Daddy, they aren't going to take you to jail, are they?"

"No, no. Where's Emile?"

Arianna said: "He's fine. He's upstairs writing in his diary."

David called the police. The detective in charge of the investigation had left for the day. David finally got through to the second-in-command. The man laughed. No, nobody was coming to arrest him, not as far as he knew.

"Well, what are these reporters doing here?"

"Beats me."

"Listen, am I a suspect or not?"

"You were the last one to leave the scene. We can't rule out anybody until our investigation is complete."

"When will that be?

"*Ah, monsieur.* Investigations take time."

Finally, after consulting with Arianna, David invited the reporters into the house and answered questions. No, the police were not coming to arrest him. No, they had not ruled him out as a suspect. No, he did not set the fire. No, he did not know how the investigation was going. No, he did not think it was going quickly enough. No, no, no.

By the time the reporters left, ninety minutes later, David felt drained. Two days before, Arianna had broached the idea of taking a leave of absence from work and bringing the children to Timmins to visit their grandmother. He'd said no way. Now, when again she suggested this, he agreed. Let the kids miss a few days of school. The furore would die down. They'd return home refreshed. Above all, they'd be safe.

The loneliness didn't hit David until he arrived back at the house after dropping off his family at Dorval airport. Then, as he walked through the front door, emptiness slammed into him like a clenched fist.

39 / THE BIG BREAK

Old Orchard Avenue, 1989. Six o'clock in the morning. Still dark outside and freezing cold. No sign yet of *The Chronicle* but David hadn't really expected it. Paper boys weren't what they used to be. He jammed the door shut, then went down the hall to the kitchen. Put coffee in the maker, bread in the toaster, wiped the counter with a damp cloth.

There, on the kitchen table, lay yesterday's *Nouvelle de Montréal.* He tossed it onto a chair and wiped the table clean. Isabelle's latest gambit. He didn't want to think about it. As he moved around the kitchen, picking up and putting away, he thought instead of a long-ago Saturday morning in Ste-Thérèse.

David was halfway down the back steps, leaving to do his newspaper collecting, when the telephone rang. His father was still in bed, though it was past noon, and his mother had gone grocery shopping, taken the kids. He dashed back inside and answered. Fraticelli wanted to speak to his father. Said it was urgent.

The old man hadn't been drinking lately, not since the family had visited Nova Scotia. But he'd stayed up late the night before, watching *Casablanca,* a favorite Humphrey Bogart movie, and David had trouble waking him: "Dad! It's your friend, Mr. Fraticelli. Wake up!"

He found himself hoping, almost praying, that Fraticelli had turned up some kind of job offer. What else could be urgent? David could see that his father was down. Forty-two years old, he'd woken up and found he had a wife and four kids. That he wasn't Humphrey Bogart, after all. He was Gerard Nelligan, formerly of *La Victoire de Bonaventure,* who couldn't find another newspapering job.

He'd begun hunting at the top, and why not? But the managing editor at *The Montreal Standard* was related to Grenier by marriage and *The Chronicle* wouldn't even look at his clippings. Didn't hire anybody who hadn't worked for a daily.

Turned down, then, by a variety of weeklies — family affairs, typically, that employed one or two people — his father took a civil-defence course sponsored by the federal government. Paid thirty-five dollars a week. Lasted two months. Then he found work with a local contractor, digging drains, installing septic tanks, raising summer camps and putting cement-block foundations under them. Fifty dollars a week. A long way from *Casablanca*.

David's mother, meanwhile, had tried working as a cleaning lady. She'd catch the Greyhound bus into Bonaventure to vacuum rugs and scrub floors and, as she put it, "clean other people's toilets." Hated it so much she decided to face commuting and landed a job as a file clerk in a Montreal insurance office.

She'd rise at five o'clock, get the wood stove going, send David out to deliver newspapers, prepare the lunches, make breakfast for the kids and coffee for his father, then take the taxi, Old Leroux, into Bonaventure and catch the train to work. When his father told her to slow down, she'd say, "Grangers have no slow-down in them."

Late summer, his father's right arm seized up. The doctor told him it was bursitis. Hard physical labor was out. No more carting cement blocks. His father stayed home and took care of the house. As summer turned to fall, he enlarged the front room by knocking down a half-wall and boarding up the front-porch windows. Then he installed a sink in the bathroom so they didn't have to brush their teeth into the bathtub.

"Clean-up brigade!" he'd cry at around four-thirty. "Twenty minutes to inspection! Look at this mess! I don't care what you do with it, get it out of sight!" And he'd lead a mad dash around the house, sweeping, fluffing pillows, tossing toys into a basket.

But his heart wasn't in it and David could see that, and so he stood listening that morning in the autumn of 1963 while his father talked on the phone with Fraticelli. He'd pulled on his tired maroon bathrobe and stood hunched over the counter that separated the kitchen from the front room, looking around for a pen.

"You used my theory? Ha! David, hand me that pencil."

His father scrawled a note and said, "See you in half an hour."

Hung up and began dashing around the house.

David said: "What's up?"

"Two guys have confessed. French guys — I was right."

"What? The Laliberté murder?"

"Fraticelli cracked the case. He's giving me an exclusive."

"Dad, you're not a reporter any more."

"We'll see about that, son. This could be the break we've been waiting for."

His father phoned the taxi, Old Leroux, and ran out the door a few minutes later: "Tell your mother not to hold supper."

It was evening when his father returned. Said he'd talked with the killers for three hours straight. They wanted to tell their story, claimed the death was accidental. "Here it is, Nellie!" He brandished his notebook. "I've got an exclusive."

"Yes, but nowhere to publish it."

"I've phoned *The Chronicle*."

"*The Chronicle?*"

"They want to see what I've got."

His father wolfed down supper, then went out into the front porch. It was still a junk shop and David could hear him digging around. Finally, he came back carrying his typewriter. "Make me a pot of coffee, Nellie, will you?"

"You're not going to start typing now?"

"This could be it, Nellie. The big one — the break we've been waiting for."

"The big one," his mother said. "We're always waiting for the big one."

But she made a pot of coffee.

Two hours later, David fell asleep to the sound of his father's rapid two-finger typing: clack clack, clackety clack clack, clackety clack clack clack.

Next day was Sunday. No newspaper. David awoke to the sound of his father talking in strange bursts, discovered he'd taken the telephone into his bedroom. In the kitchen, to his mother, David said, "What's he doing?"

"Dictating the story he wrote."

His father remained on the phone for forty minutes. Finally hung up and came into the kitchen, exhausted but happy: "That's it."

David's mother said, "Are they going to run it?"

"Are they going to run it?" His father looked at the ceiling. "Are they going to run it?" He poured himself a coffee. "Actually, she didn't know, the woman who transcribed it. But don't worry, they'll run it."

Next morning, when David got up to deliver *the Chronicles*, he found his father at the kitchen table, reading the paper. His story, complete with pictures, took up half the front page: "Auto workers confess to murder." A sidebar headline said: "Bonaventure cop uses reporter's theory to crack case."

"Check the byline," his father said.

David read it aloud: "By Gerard Nelligan. Special to *The Chronicle*." He looked up. "Does this mean they're going to give you a job?"

"We'll see, son."

Two days later, his father went to see *The Chronicle*'s managing editor, a cigar-chomping Irishman named Hennessey.

Later, he'd taken David and his mother through the scene a dozen times.

"You did a fine job on that murder," Hennessey said. "But we're over-staffed."

"What about down the road? Any chance a reporting job will come open?"

Hennessey leaned back in his chair, put his feet up on his desk and blew a smoke ring. "Tell me, Gerry. What do you know about Cornwall?"

"Cornwall, Ontario? It's a pulp and paper town."

"Friend of mine's launching a weekly there. If you like, I'll give him a call."

"Gee, I don't know, Mr. Hennessey. Montreal's my home. I was born and raised here."

"Think about it, Gerry. Let me know."

David's father didn't have to think about it.

He quit hunting newspaper jobs, began investigating public relations. Found work, eventually, with Canadian Guaranty Life.

40 / WRONG QUESTION

Newspaperless, David turned to his sporadic journal, early 1976. Began reading and shook his head. Over the years, enemies had called him impatient, arrogant, egotistical. They'd called him cavalier. But nobody had ever said "lost and floundering." Nobody had ever said "in over his head." This exploration was proving more cathartic than he'd anticipated.

> *Isabelle blathers on, oblivious to anybody but herself. I go upstairs after coffee break without once having touched her, say, "See you later." Maybe she's not unaware but simply can't cope. Too many demands. Writing. Workshops. Her political group. Now Greek lessons. Yes. But it's being at the bottom of the list that I resent.*
>
> *I go for long walks, as I did with Arianna. Only now I go alone. I'm not sorry I chose "the road less travelled," but I begin to see what I gave up. Isabelle says that what I really need is someone to BE THERE constantly. Which is childish.*
>
> *Still, I'd like to have someone to talk with once in a while. Share my feelings. With Isabelle, one can only listen. The question remains: What to do?*

A portrait of the artist as a young cry-baby, David thought now. The entry revealed his loneliness but skirted what Isabelle knew to be the real issue: his continuing relationship with Arianna. David met her weekly to exchange the Volkswagen. They could no longer stroll comfortably on Mount Royal — too cold, too much snow — so instead they swam at the Claude Robillard Centre in the north end.

During these outings, David rarely said a word about what he was enduring with Isabelle. But one night he did mention that when Kurt left her, she'd thrown insane temper tantrums and stormed uninvited into dinner parties to denounce former friends as "cheats" and "husband-stealers." Arianna said she, too, had felt angry — and so depressed sometimes that she hadn't wanted to get out of bed. "You know what kept me going? My childhood. I'd remember how cosy everything was, how loving. I'd remember skiing at Sunshine Village or Kamiscotia and think: 'I can have that again.'"

Later, as David came through the front door in Outremont, Isabelle emerged into the living room speaking English. "Did you have a nice swim? Did your itty-bitty wife out-swim you again? Oh, poor baby."

Usually, David answered her sarcasm with laughter. He'd explain that since Isabelle didn't like to swim, these outings took nothing away from their relationship. This time, as he hung up his coat, he said: "Knock it off, Isabelle. I have a right to a life of my own."

"You're living with me, you English blockhead. I want you to stop dating your wife."

"I'm not English. I'm Irish and French and Mohawk. And we've got to exchange the Volkswagen, remember? What's the big deal? Every time I turn around, you're out lunching with some man."

"That's different. Those men are my friends."

"No way I'll stop seeing Arianna." He started away up the stairs. "That's that."

"Don't you dare turn your back on me!" Isabelle ran up the stairs and smashed her fist into his back.

He spun around and said coldly: "Don't you ever do that again." Then turned and resumed climbing.

Later, in bed, they made up. But David couldn't help thinking that he and Arianna had never been reduced to blows and threats. Hadn't even come close, not in five years. And the journal entries kept coming.

Amazing but true, I've built this relationship on lies. This weekend Isabelle let slip that she slept with T.J. for the last time while Arianna and I were in New York. Until now she always insisted that she didn't sleep with him then because I'd asked her not to. So, here she was in Montreal, balling both T.J. and Jacques Bienvenue, while I was agonizing in New York about a stalled Volkswagen.

I remember when I got back, Isabelle gave me a long letter. Talked about sleeping with Bienvenue "for old time's sake." T.J. she didn't mention, but before giving me the letter, she did ask me what was

*wrong. We were standing outside that coffee shop on Laurier. I told
her, "T.J." Asked if she'd seen him. She said she had, but insisted she
hadn't slept with him. "Don't lie to me," I said. "If you lie and I find
out...."*

"I'm not lying," she said.

*But she was. Now she admits it and here I am, still around,
wondering why she lies all the time? Compulsive? If she'd told me about
T.J. back then, I might have come to my senses. Pulled out. Instead,
here I sit. I called her a cheat and a liar. She cried and then dragged
me to bed.*

Now, reading this journal entry on Old Orchard Avenue, David
wanted to reach across Time and shake the young man who'd
written it, shout: "Never mind why Isabelle lied, you fool! Ask
yourself why, after all this time, she let slip the truth!"

41 / CONFESSION OVER-RULED

"If things were so terrible, David, why didn't you walk away?" So the voice inside him as he rambled the empty house.

Coldly, into the silence, David said: "We've already gone over that."

"Yes, but what was your self-talk? How did you rationalize your behaviour? How did you justify hurting not just yourself but others?"

"Is that you, Arianna?"

"Wishful thinking, David."

"You sound just like her — your tone, your inflections. Your attitude."

"Why didn't you walk away? I'll tell you. Because all your life you wanted secretly to be French. To be *Québécois pure laine.*"

"The French thing was part of it."

"Isabelle was your bid for acceptance. If you could make it with her —"

He picked up his bongos: "Let's give it a rest."

"David, we're just beginning. You wanted to be a writer, remember? But you were naive. Believed suffering creates The Artist. That the more intensely you suffered, the greater you'd become."

"If my vocation demanded suffering, then yes, I was ready to suffer."

"And to make others suffer, as well."

David began thumping away on his bongos, but had trouble finding the rhythm he wanted. The voice kept coming: "You say you feared Isabelle."

"You've got that straight."

"But maybe you loved her, too."

"Early on, I was infatuated. But I never loved Isabelle. I survived her."

"Maybe so. But that's NOT what you told yourself. You insisted that you loved two women. That was how you justified your disgraceful behaviour — not only to yourself, but to anybody who'd listen."

"Green, green — I was green!"

Trouble was, David realized, finding the groove, Isabelle had been hard enough on herself in *Le Diable Entre Nous* — "yes, I was hungry for love" — that she'd fostered an illusion of truth. And he couldn't demonstrate the extent of her duplicity unless he lied to himself less than she'd done.

He remembered how, early in 1976, he asked Arianna what she wanted for her birthday. She said, "I want to ski with you at Mont Tremblant."

A day alone in the mountains? Isabelle would go nuts. But David was desperate to spend time with Arianna. He embraced the idea. After all, what was one day? Maybe he could sell it.

But no. Isabelle was outraged. She ranted, called him a selfish, spoiled brat. He said he'd promised and couldn't back out. They'd already set a date.

The following week, Isabelle asked him to change the date so he could attend a reading she'd been invited to give. Said his presence was important to her. David phoned Arianna and changed the date. A few days later, Isabelle asked him to change it again: Chantal Leclerc, an expatriate writer friend, would be visiting from France. She wanted them to meet.

David admired Leclerc's work, but he wasn't about to seek another change. He told Isabelle he'd arrive home in time for a late dinner and meet her friend then. Eventually, despite her fury, her ranting about his selfishness, that's what he did. And he enjoyed meeting Leclerc — though it wasn't the highlight of the day.

That came at Mont Tremblant, where the weather was a cliché of perfection: bright sunshine, not a cloud in the sky. Six inches of powder had fallen the night before. Because it was a weekday, the crowds were thin. Even Arianna, who remembered skiing the Rockies, pronounced conditions perfect.

At noon they stopped for lunch. Sat outside the lodge in wooden chairs, drinking coffee, gorging themselves on hotdogs and fries. David thought of Isabelle, back home in Montreal, talking literature with Chantal Leclerc. Yes, he would have enjoyed being there. But Mont Tremblant was blue sky, perfect snow — and Arianna. As he sat basking, David realized that this was where he wanted to be. And awoke to the corollary: This was the woman he wanted to be with.

That was the moment. There on Mont Tremblant.

David didn't act on that moment until the following Friday, when he met Arianna to exchange the Volkswagen. They'd swam, eaten smoked meat sandwiches at Ben's Delicatessan, and now sat talking out front of her apartment. Neither of them wanted to say good-night. Finally, David leaned over and kissed her. When Arianna kissed him back, he asked if he could come upstairs.

They made love and David wept — though he couldn't have explained why. Arianna held him and stroked his head, and when he sat up, David found himself in an enchanted garden, alone with the woman he loved. Even the crumpled sheets looked beautiful. He said: "Do you see what I see, Arianna?"

"It feels like the Garden of Eden."

That night, back in Outremont, David slept badly. But next morning, when he awoke, he knew what he had to do. Isabelle had gone to her cabin in Ste-Adèle. Her boys were visiting, and she'd driven them up the previous afternoon, while he'd stayed in Mont-real to teach an English class. He'd planned to drive north via the back highways, enjoying the Laurentians in winter: small towns, frozen lakes, snow-covered mountains.

As he drove, though, David saw nothing. All he could think about was what he had to do. At the cabin, Isabelle sat reading by the woodstove in the kitchen. Her boys were out skating on the lake. David brought groceries into the house, and two armloads of wood, and then asked Isabelle to join him in the big main room.

"I can't go to Greece with you, Isabelle."

"What are you talking about?"

"I can't go."

"You made a commitment. You have to go."

"I still love Arianna."

Isabelle sat him down on the edge of the bed: "Of course you still love her. But you also love me."

"I can't leave Arianna."

"You've already left her."

"No, I haven't."

"You can't back out now, David. We've bought the freighter tickets."

"We can send them back."

"Not without taking an impossible loss."

"We'll split the loss."

"You can't back out, David. You gave me your word. Besides, I need you more than she does. I need you to synthesize my crazy fragments. I need your laughter and your love. I need your body." While she talked, Isabelle stroked his hair, the back of his neck. "I know you've been unhappy. It's been hard this year, having my friends around and with all these ghosts. But you and I have never really been alone."

Isabelle caressed his thighs. "Think of it, David. No work demands, no political friends. Just the two of us, sitting in a villa looking out over the Mediterranean. And before that, the freighter cruise! We'll visit the Canary Islands, David. Barcelona, Genoa, Naples. Say the names, David. The names are magic."

"Isabelle, I still love Arianna."

"We've never had a chance, David. You owe me a chance."

No such scene turned up in *Le Diable Entre Nous*. There, the relentlessly honest Isabelle Garneau had plenty to say about her anti-hero's Anglophone obtuseness. But not one word about his attempts to communicate the truth. His efforts to escape. Her refusal to let him go.

42 / THE WAJADILI TWIST

Separating from Arianna had been one thing. Sailing to Greece without her would be another. David didn't think he could do it. He took longer walks. He drank more red wine. He continued to see Arianna and fight with Isabelle about it. Only now when he denied that he'd been sleeping with his wife, he was lying.

Arianna, meanwhile, had sent out dozens of job applications. She was completing her second degree and hoped to find design work in a foreign country. She'd been reduced to considering an offer from an outfit in British Columbia, though, when lightning struck.

David was marking essays the night Arianna phoned. Her voice shaking with excitement, she said she'd received a telegram from Africa — the Republic of Wajadili. A Canadian company was building an office complex in the capital city, Kalinda. They were offering her a one-year contract. They'd pay travel expenses and, when she completed the contract, they'd throw in a bonus.

"You going to accept?"

"Are you kidding?"

When, ten minutes later, David hung up the phone, he took five deep breaths. And then five more. He dug out his Atlas and located Wajadili. East Africa. There, on the same map, was Greece. The Atlas open in front of him, David opened a drawer, took out a bottle of wine and knocked back two quick glasses.

Realized he couldn't sit still. Isabelle was in the basement, some political meeting, and David tip-toed through the house. He put on his duffle coat and boots and went out the front door. The night was cold and clear. He walked down the path, swung onto the sidewalk and broke into a trot.

Arianna had landed a job in Africa — and she was certain he could do the same! The telegram mentioned a strong Canadian presence in the capital city of Kalinda. David ran up one street and down the next. The gods were smiling on him, after all. He could go to Greece, as Isabelle insisted. And he wouldn't have to look back in anguish. Instead, he could look ahead with anticipation. Arianna had landed a job in Africa!

David didn't tell Isabelle right away. Two days later, when he broke the news, he had his answers ready. Yes, he did intend to visit Arianna in Wajadili. No, he didn't know what he would do then. How could he know?

During the next few days, Isabelle articulated her reaction in both official languages. She didn't object to his visiting Arianna, but to being presented with a *fait accompli*. Why one standard of behaviour for him and another for her? "If I'd come to you with an announcement like this," she said, "you'd have yelled and screamed and accused me, in English of course, of "having hot-pants" or "can't get enough" or some other charming expression. It's the same old double standard."

"Isabelle, if you want to call off Greece, just say so."

She wanted no such thing, of course.

Towards the end of May, after classes ended, she mounted a last-ditch offensive: "You know, David, you haven't changed your attitude towards women since the sixties." She'd walked into the bedroom when he was on the phone to Arianna. "I'm not saying you don't 'love' me or Arianna, but you also want to use us. We're your guarantee that you'll have sympathetic listeners and bed-partners."

"You don't listen, Isabelle. You talk."

"You've got it all figured out, haven't you, David?" She began pacing, talking to the ceiling. "In August, when I'm at the cabin in Ste-Adele, working, you'll be here in Montreal, ostensibly lining up freelance work — but really spending time with Arianna. In September, you'll travel to Greece with me. Come Christmas, you'll become the solitary adventurer, a notebook in one pocket, a snake-bite kit in the other, travelling down the Nile to see your Other Woman — your wife. Spend some time with her, maybe even stay, who knows?"

"Isabelle, I phoned Arianna to find out when her plane leaves."

"Arianna will have a place set up and know her way around. You can tell her about Greece and your trip down the Nile. I'll get a postcard with Thomson's gazelles on the outside. 'Having a wonderful time.' But not, 'Wish you were here.' Oh, no. You think it's funny, David? It would be different if you were operating from a neutral base of your own. To make it fair, you should have a place in a foreign country that Arianna and I want to visit."

"I had to know when she's leaving."

"I really do think you can't change your attitude towards women. That's why I say to hell with any promises you've made to me. They're just empty words. You'll get around them, somehow. You'll always have a ready excuse like, 'I had to know when she's leaving.'"

David picked up his pillow and walked out the door. Down the stairs he went and out the back door to his study, where he had a cot. Isabelle followed, yelling. "Don't run away, David. When you went out on your bicycle yesterday, you probably rode over to see Arianna. It's impossible for you to leave her alone."

"Get out of my study, please."

"I won't get out. This is my house."

"Say what you like, then, Isabelle. Go ahead, rave until you're blue in the face. Bottom line? I'll go to Greece, as promised. But come Christmas, I'm going to Africa."

43 / OBLIGATORY SCENE

Arianna arrived in Greece wearing an African skirt of many colours. Tanned and fit and lovely, she took my breath away. She'd been jogging daily, she reminded me, early mornings around Kalinda. She laughed at my consternation and I remembered how it used to be. How could I have let her go?

We rode the airport bus downtown, brought her luggage to the Hotel Cleo, then went to a nearby taverna for a late dinner. The taverna had no name but I'd scouted it carefully: candles, red-checked table cloths, an older man in a brown sports jacket who wandered among the customers playing a guitar and singing love songs. Arianna pronounced the place enchanting.

We drank red wine while she talked about the office complex she was helping to design. She showed me her sketchbook: women with baskets on their heads, children playing at the ocean, carvers at work under thatched roofs. Some of the best work she'd done. I talked about my novel-in-progress, about the Quebec election — she'd heard only the result — and, finally, about Isabelle, who was still insisting that we all three spend Chrismas together.

Why? Because she's compelled, I see now, to live an experience before she writes it. That's her notion of authenticity. She needed a crescendo to end the novel she was living, a climax that revealed me as a diabolical sorcerer. Let's face it: she couldn't end her fantasy with her heroine begging that Nasty Anglo Male to help her leave Apolakia — especially not after he'd caught her copying his private letters.

In Athens, of course, I lacked even this much clarity. But I explained as best I could and Arianna stroked my hand. "Just relax, David. Stop worrying, okay?"

We ate souvlaki and drank too much wine. And later that night, back at the Hotel Cleo, we found the magic garden that was ours and I wondered yet again how I ever could have left.

For the next few days, Arianna and I played tourist. We visited the ruins at Delphi, found no trace of the oracle, and travelled further north. Here I have a photo of the two of us in Meteora, laughing together out front of a medieval monastery. It's perched atop one of those incredible, hoodoo-like towers of rock that have made the site famous — fantastic black mushrooms jutting hundreds of feet into the sky. Arianna wears an ankle-length rain cape, though the sun shines brightly, because for women slacks were prohibited. Too arousing.

Of the three of us together in Greece, I've turned up a single photograph. A professional took it, a man who specialized in shooting tourists visiting the Acropolis and used an elaborate Instamatic mounted on a tripod. We're seated on a fallen column, the Parthenon behind us, our faces strained.

I sit in the middle, my legs crossed at the ankles, my hands in my lap. On my right, Arianna wears a fireman's cape she'd found in a second-hand store, and which she needed because of the relative cold. Isabelle sits on my left, her black hair peeking out from beneath a tam, the split in her face pronounced.

We posed for the photo on Christmas Eve, late afternoon. We'd eaten a picnic lunch in the ruins of the Lyceum, down below, then climbed the hill to admire the Parthenon. We were trying to get along.

Two days before, on returning from Meteora, Arianna and I had made a mistake. Isabelle had pointed out that the lower level of the rooming house on Poukakos street had three separate rooms — two besides hers. Both now vacant. Why didn't Arianna and I rent them? Much cheaper than staying at a hotel.

Foolishly, we'd gone along with this.

Since our return, we'd eaten dinner together, all three of us, in one of the roaring, over-crowded tavernas of the Plaka, where we stuffed our faces with moussaka and drank too much retsina. At one point Isabelle broached the subject of sisterhood and bonding between women and Arianna had stared at her and changed the subject.

Next day, in the bustling, pre-Christmas streets around Syntagma Square, the three of us wolfed down donairs, munched hot roasted chestnuts and bought lottery tickets at every second kiosk. We kept things superficial, though, and by the time we had our photos taken on the Acropolis, the strain was showing.

Christmas provided both distraction and focus: parcels to wrap, food to prepare. Out walking by herself on the evening we moved into the house, Arianna discovered some small Christmas trees for sale and, on impulse, bought one. Dragged it home through the streets. She and I set it up in the downstairs hall and decorated it with what we could find: cards from home, mostly, and a few Greek doodads from each of our rooms.

On Christmas Eve, the three of us joined the upstairs roomers for a turkey dinner laid on by the landlord and his wife. Next morning, sitting around the tree, we traded gifts. From Wajadili, Arianna had brought two batiked shirts for me, and for Isabelle, a colorful wrap-around skirt. I gave Arianna a Greek dress and oil paints, and Isabelle a leather briefcase and a gorgeous vase. Isabelle had spent less money, though we pretended not to notice: for Arianna, a sketch book, and for me, a leather belt.

Somehow, we got through Christmas.

And that's where, in *Le Diable Entre Nous*, Isabelle leaves her readers. She cut to the present for a poor-me soliloquoy. One reviewer, at least, had the wit to wonder: "Where's the final rupture? The obligatory scene?"

Answer: that came on Boxing Day. After lunch, Arianna suggested that the three of us go for a long walk, maybe climb one of the city's major hills. Isabelle said no thanks, she wanted to be alone — and fair enough. Arianna and I climbed Lycabettus, then wandered around the Plaka, bought milk and feta cheese and black olives. When we got back to the house, early evening, Isabelle was sitting in her room with the door open. She'd been drinking ouzo and said it was time the three of us had a talk.

It didn't take a clairvoyant to spot the heavy-weather signals and I said: "Let's talk tomorrow."

Isabelle insisted. Arianna made herself comfortable. After putting the groceries in the fridge down the hall, I joined the two women. Isabelle wanted to talk about the previous afternoon. I'd upset her, she said, by drinking wine with that young Australian woman, an upstairs roomer, while she and Arianna prepared lunch.

True, I later did the dishes alone, and also cleaned the kitchen. Even so, my behaviour had been chauvinistic, Isabelle said, and she'd been furious — though until now she'd said nothing.

"Isabelle, I'm exhausted," I said. "Can't this wait until tomorrow?"

"Getting together was your idea, David. Now you want to sit back and let the women make it work."

"My idea? You torpedoed my idea, Isabelle, when you moved here to Athens. This was your idea."

"Maybe we should call it a night," Arianna said. "Shouting at each other won't solve anything."

"Go ahead, take his side. You don't surprise me — Mrs. Nelligan!"

Isabelle was alluding to Christmas Eve dinner. At the table upstairs, with six or seven nationalities represented, we'd started talking — innocently enough, I thought — about origins and surnames. Or maybe our British hostess did steer the conversation. Point blank, anyway, she asked Arianna: "And what's your last name?"

Arianna said, "Nelligan."

"Why, that's David's name."

"Yes, we share the same last name."

Perhaps, as Isabelle suggested, Arianna could have answered, "Larivière." But for five years she'd used Nelligan. And what about her passport? The tags on her suitcase? She didn't add, "He's my husband."

Yet that exchange, Isabelle said, hurt her deeply. If we all three shared a house, Arianna and I would be Mr. and Mrs. Nelligan. "But where do I fit in?"

Arianna said, "Who's talking about sharing a house?"

"So that's how it is!" Isabelle said. "You two never intended to make this work."

"Eh bien, c'est assez pour un soir," Arianna said. "I'm hitting the sack."

Isabelle yelled: "You sit down!"

At the door, Arianna stopped and said coolly: "Who do you think you're talking to, Isabelle? David?"

Then she walked out.

Isabelle jumped to her feet and ran into the hall. "Don't you walk away from me, you bitch! Better still, why don't you just keep walking? Go on, get out of my house!"

"This isn't your house, Isabelle. But don't worry. You won't have to suggest that twice."

I said, "Arianna, wait."

"You do what what you want, David. I'm going to a hotel."

"If you're leaving, so am I."

Imitating Arianna's voice, Isabelle said: "You do what you want, David. You do what you want, I'm going to a hotel." Back in her own voice, she yelled: "When you know damn well he's going to follow you out the door! You hypocritical bitch!"

Looking around for something to throw, Isabelle spotted the Greek vase I'd given her for Christmas. She grabbed it and hurled it down the hall, smashing it to pieces against the front door. "You never had any intention, either of you, of trying to make this work. Go on, get out!"

Isabelle looked around for something else to throw. Spotting the Christmas tree, on which Arianna had worked so hard, she ran over and jerked it out of its stand. "Get out of my house!"

Holding the tree near its top end, swinging it like a baseball bat, Isabelle smashed it into the front door. Decorations went flying. "Lying hypocrites!" Again she smashed the tree into the door. "This is my house! I found it! And I'm telling you to get out! Go on, get out!" Again she smashed the tree into the door. "Get out! Get out!"

She was still swinging the tree when the landlord burst through the door: "Isabelle, what's happening?"

He eyed me suspiciously and I shrugged: "She gets like this."

The landlord invited Isabelle upstairs for coffee. She refused, but he insisted, took her by the arm and led her gently away.

Arianna went into her room and began packing. "You do what you want, David. But I'm leaving."

"I'm leaving with you."

I swept the front hall clean of debris and broken glass, then went to my room and dug out my rucksack. We were both still packing when Isabelle returned, much subdued. She went straight into her bedroom. After a few moments, in a small, quavering voice, she began calling my name.

Finally, at Arianna's insistence, I went to her. Isabelle lay curled up in bed. She'd been hallucinating, she said. Earlier that evening, she'd seen me turn into her ex-husband, Kurt. Then she'd seen me as the devil, as Satan himself. Now I looked like me again. She begged me not to leave her alone — not tonight. Not with that gas burner in her room. If I left, she didn't know what she might do.

I crossed the hall and Arianna told me I'd better stay the night.

"I'm not staying unless you stay."

"All right. I'll stay until morning."

I cuddled Isabelle through the night.

Early next morning I rose and crossed the hall. Arianna was already out of bed and preparing to leave. I finished packing. When I looked in on Isabelle, she pretended to be asleep. Arianna and I laid our keys on the trunk and let ourselves out of the house.

44 / THINGS FALL APART

Having transformed all of Greece into a pile of printed pages, David finally had to admit what he'd begun to suspect the previous evening. His Big Idea didn't stand up. Ethnic nationalists wanted to drive Anglophones out of the province. *Le Québec aux Québécois.* Isabelle, on the other hand, had refused to let him go. In Athens, even after driving him and Arianna out of the rooming house, she'd tracked him down and begged him to remain in Greece. Cited yet another original agreement.

Even in his arrogance, furthermore, David had to admit that his mid-twenties self exemplified Quebec's English community in only one particular: his painful naiveté. And where did Arianna fit? Canada minus Quebec was many things, but half-French and profoundly empathetic it was not. On Old Orchard Avenue, David pushed away from his computer. Another writer might be able to fashion these echoes and reflections into a political allegory. But the task was beyond him.

He snatched *The Chronicle* from the coffee table — it had arrived around six-thirty — and stared again at Page B1. Isabelle's gambit. The story was a translation, almost word-for-word, of the piece that had run in *La Nouvelle de Montréal*. Foolishly, he'd been hoping against hope. But this, he knew, his crediblity could never survive. And when Isabelle's novel appeared in translation? Already Arianna had been having second thoughts about rebuilding in Montreal.

David tossed *The Chronicle* onto the coffee table, went to the window and drew aside the curtain. Down the street, two of the original three people were still trying to wrestle their van out of the snow. Surely they hadn't been at it all night? No, they must have quit when the snowplow buried the vehicle a second time, then started again this morning.

David let the curtain fall and glanced at his watch. Seven-twenty. Too early to call Timmins. Yet he felt a need to act, to do something. He went to the hall cupboard, took out his duffle coat and pulled it on. Then, while lacing up his workboots, he looked around at the files and papers and boxes and briefly considered throwing the whole mess into the fireplace. Fought down this impulse.

Pulling on his tuque, David went out the back door and locked it shut behind him. The day was cold enough that, even in the grey light of morning, he could see his breath. He waded through eight inches of snow and entered the garage through a side door. It was a converted quonset hut, a neighborhood eyesore, but it kept his rattletrap Chevy snow-free and warm.

After twice pressing his foot to the floor, David turned the key and the old car roared to life. Automatically, because the fuel gauge didn't work, he asked himself when he'd last filled the gas tank. Three days before the storm? Four? Unable to remember, and knowing the Chevy had to warm up anyway, David climbed out of the car. He opened the trunk, reached in and hefted a plastic, two-gallon container. It felt full.

Reassured, David put it away and climbed back into the car. As he swung out onto Old Orchard, he saw that where the van had been, now there was a gaping hole in the snowbank. This, he told himself, this was an omen.

David headed east along Sherbrooke. Traffic was light but the street was slippery and he not only stopped at red lights but slowed down for green ones. Atwater, Guy, Mountain, Peel. David turned left up Aylmer, then left again onto Milton. Just before he came to the bookstore, still boarded up, he swung right up the alley, pulled over and parked.

At the back door, his hands cold, David fumbled with the padlock, finally made it work. He entered the store and flicked on the light. Several times since the firebombing, he'd visited this burnt-out shell. But he'd never adjusted to the transformation. Now, again, he reacted viscerally, felt both sick and angry at the charred walls and shelves and the lingering smell of burnt books.

From the wall behind his desk a cardboard sign proclaimed: "Calypso 101 lives!" He'd hung it there two days after the fire-bombing, when he'd visited these charred remains for the first time. The perfect prop for his televised press conference. Sheer bravado, he realized now. Bravado and self-delusion. His civil disobedience campaign had collapsed when the arson rumors started. Though maybe he could resuscitate it?

Almost eight o'clock. Still too early to call, but David couldn't stop himself. He went to his desk, picked up the telephone — he'd insisted on keeping it connected — and dialed Timmins from memory. Arianna's mother answered. Something in his voice cut short her greeting. Then Arianna was on the line. He told her he missed her.

"You didn't call me at this hour to tell me that."

"When are you coming home?" His voice cracked. "I need you, Arianna. You and the kids. How are the kids?"

"The kids are fine. They're still in bed. It's Isabelle, isn't it? That wretched book coming out in English."

This stunned him into silence.

Arianna continued: "It's in the *Globe* this morning. David, why didn't you tell me?"

"I was afraid you wouldn't want to come home. To live here again, I mean."

"We survived that horrible novel in French, David. But you're right. I don't think we can do it in English — not in Montreal. What's important is that we stick together as a family. Rebuild somewhere else."

"You mean abandon the bookstore?" David looked around at the devastation. "I've been thinking about reviving the campaign."

"The campaign's dead, David. You're not a politician. You've never been happy except when you're writing."

"I haven't written for years."

"Not since Isabelle's novel appeared, I know. But in trying to destroy you, she's freed you. What have you got to lose?"

"That was my first impulse. To write an allegory about the whole dirty business. But nothing meshes."

"You need time, David. And a change of scenery. Let's move to Calgary or Vancouver. I'll start my own business."

"That's what the nationalists want. We can't let them drive us out."

"We can't stay in Montreal, David. Not with that novel coming in English."

"Daddy! Daddy, is that you?"

Emile had picked up another extension.

For ten minutes, then, David talked with the children. Heard again that they'd visited the local ski hill, Kamiscotia. Told them he missed them, he'd see them again soon. Arianna took control just before he broke down. Told him to stop worrying.

But even after he hung up, her conviction rang in his ears: "We can't stay in Montreal, David. Not with that novel coming in English."

David picked up the broom, began sweeping the floor. He tried to imagine leaving his past, changing his future. Back he came to Isabelle's novel. The attention it would receive when it appeared in English. David stopped sweeping, looked around at the charred bookstore. And heard a familiar silent ringing. Felt himself slip into that dream state in which Time stood still.

From the wall behind his desk, the cardboard sign shouted: "Calypso 101 lives!" David swallowed his anger. But this time it wouldn't say down. Moving in slow motion, he strode to the desk, reached up and pulled the sign from the wall. He ripped it in half, and then into four, and tossed the pieces onto a black pile of burnt books.

Calypso 101 was dead. Face it. Already, Isabelle had destroyed most of his credibility. Translated, her vicious novel would finish the job. So that now, even winning the libel suit against *La Nouvelle* would do him no good. Who'd want to identify with a discredited Anglo?

Dimly, David discerned the rudiments of a plan. With Isabelle, he'd been too proud to walk away. His pride had kept him with her long after he should have left. His pride? No. Face it. His fear had undone him. But now, at last, he feared her no more. As Arianna said: What did he have to lose?

The ringing stopped. David hadn't spoken to Isabelle since she'd published *Le Diable*. Even so, snapping back into real time, he picked up the telephone and dialed her number from memory. Isabelle answered, sleepily, on third ring. *"Allo?"*

David took a beat, then spoke in English: "It was you, wasn't it? You and those friends of yours set the fire."

"Hello? Who is this?"

"Get out of that house. You and anybody else. Get out now."

"David? David, is that —"

He slammed down the phone.

Certain now of what he had to do, moving with authority, David flicked off the lights. He left the charred bookstore the way he'd entered, pad-locked the door behind him. No way he'd leave Montreal. Here he could see where his father had played kick-the-can in the alley, or climb Mount Royal and, like his grandfather, stand looking out at the skyline of the city.

Before getting into his Chevy, David opened into the trunk and retrieved the plastic container of gasoline. This he placed on the front seat. He climbed into the car, turned the key and smiled grimly as, despite the cold, the Chevy roared to life. No way Isabelle was going to drive him out of Montreal.

Travelling north up Park Avenue, heading for Outremont, David began to laugh and pound the steering wheel with both hands. He knew how to enter the study out back, how to jiggle the latch, and also that Isabelle stored her papers there — decades worth of manuscripts. Now that he'd started, David couldn't stop laughing. No way Isabelle was going to drive him out of Montreal. No way she was going to destroy him.

45 / A CALYPSO CRESCENDO

Back in the house on Old Orchard Avenue, David turned to his bongo drums for release. He settled into a driving Calypso rhythm and found himself improvising, singing about how he'd arrived at the house in Outremont and discovered Isabelle standing on the front porch, flapping her arms against the cold. He jumped out of the Chevy, but instead of grabbing his plastic container full of gasoline, David scooped up two handfuls of snow and created a tight snowball.

This, with a curse, he hurled at Isabelle.

At the last moment, she ducked. He'd thrown too high anyway. Two metres above her head, the snowball smacked harmlessly into the house. Satisfied, David jumped back into the Chevy. In his rearview mirror, as he drove away, he watched Isabelle shake her fist in fury.

Later that day, Isabelle re-emerged from her house carrying a step ladder and accompanied by a photographer from *La Nouvelle de Montréal*. They intended to get a shot of her pointing at the remains of The Notorious Nelligan's snowball.

Because of the cold, Isabelle hurried to get into position and have done. She climbed onto the ladder without first wiping snow from her feet. On the third rung, she slipped. She might have regained her balance, but no, she fell from the ladder. She might have landed unhurt in the snow, jumped up and brushed herself off. But no. She smacked her head on the photographer's tripod and knocked herself cold.

Isabelle never did regain consciousness. She lapsed into a coma. Two days later, she died.

The photographer, who had his own worries, fudged details of the accident and made sure the snowball story never saw print. Several newspapers did run obituaries, however, and two hundred people turned up for Isabelle's funeral. David Nelligan read all about it.

"David, have you gone crazy?" So the voice inside him. "Tell the truth!"

Slapping away on his bongos, David cried: "Mighty Hamlet's the name! You can't win a Calypso War without taking casualties!"

"But Isabelle lives! You tried to burn her house down."

Flailing madly, David threw back his head and laughed at the ceiling: "Don't believe everything you read in the papers."

"The police arrived just in time."

Several months went by, and still David heard nothing about any English translation of *Le Diable Entre Nous*. Finally, he asked around and determined that the would-be translator had interpreted Isabelle's death as a portent. She'd taken her grant money and moved to Poland.

"The translation appeared. Attracted all kinds of attention. Mighty Hamlet, come back!"

Meanwhile, at police headquarters, senior officers realized that they'd behaved badly. They didn't solve the bookstore arson, and never would, but they did publicly absolve David Nelligan of any involvement. As a result, the insurance company shelled out almost enough money to open a new bookstore. *La Nouvelle de Montréal* came up with the rest, settling the libel suit out of court by paying David an amount of money he agreed never to divulge.

Arianna talked about taking this $100,000 and moving out West. But with Isabelle dead and no translation in the works, she proposed this half-heartedly. Both she and the children rejoiced at the compromise David suggested: open a bookstore in the Eastern Townships — less than two hours from downtown Montreal. Yes, that's where they created it: Calypso Canada Too.

"Arianna waited as long as she could for you to come around. Then she took the kids and moved to Calgary."

Creating a bookstore, David discovered, was easier second time around. And, surprise: he even found time to write fiction. He set aside the rough notes he'd punched out on Old Orchard and erased Isabelle from his mind. Instead of writing about Greece, he told a magical story that shunted between Quebec and a fictional African nation that boasted thirty-five languages. Having abandoned the notion of allegory, he opted for tangled complexity, drew on personal experience and let the novel tell itself.

When he was satisfied, David shipped the manuscript to a hot-shot New York agent, why not? Three weeks later, he got a phone call. The agent not only loved the book, but had already solicited an offer from a major international publisher: Would David accept an advance of five hundred thousand dollars?

Nine months later, when the novel appeared, it was hailed all over the world. David was especially gratified by the response of French Quebec. *Le Journal de Montréal* called the work "a literary miracle," while *La Presse* spoke of its "stunning transformative power." *Le Devoir* likened the book to "a thunderbolt on the road to Damascus." The premier of the province read the novel at a single sitting, and the following week he renounced his decades-old nationalism and invited David Nelligan to redesign Quebec's language policy.

David regretfully declined, explaining that he'd already made plans to travel for a year with Arianna and the children. But he convinced the provincial government to appoint Emmanuel Tolbert in his stead, and was well-pleased with the results. His novel went on to win several awards, both at home and abroad, and reliable sources tell him that, any day now, he can expect a call from Hollywood.

"That's pathetic. Does The Mighty Hamlet have nothing serious to add?"

For a few seconds more, David wailed away on his bongos. He brought his flailing to an ecstatic frenzy, a Calypso crescendo, and then whap! Sudden silence. "A moral you want?" David shrugged and grinned lopsidedly into the camera. "Don't run away to Greece with one of the immortals. It might take you forever to sort out the mess."